THE
TORCH BEARER'S
EXORCISM

Also By LLVT:

SPANISH ANGST:
What I Wish I'd Known BEFORE I Moved to Madrid

THE TORCH BEARER'S EXORCISM

LINDA LUISA VARELA TYCHSEN

ARPress
45 Dan Road Suite 15
Canton MA 02021

Hotline:	1(888) 821-0229
Fax:	1(508) 545-7580

Ordering Information:
Quantity sales. Special discounts are available on quantity purchases by corporations, associations, and others. For details, contact the publisher at the address above.

Printed in the United States of America.

ISBN-13:	Softcover	979-8-89356-948-3
	eBook	979-8-89356-950-6
	Hardback	979-8-89356-949-0

Library of Congress Control Number: 2019920185

This is for my dear commie bagel Stanislav Berkovich who knew me better than me when I was new to it all; was right about every man I got involved with although I never paid any mind, and told me a long time ago that I should do this.

Stan's untimely death at 33 left me without a confidant and he is still very much loved and missed by this half breed Euro trash.

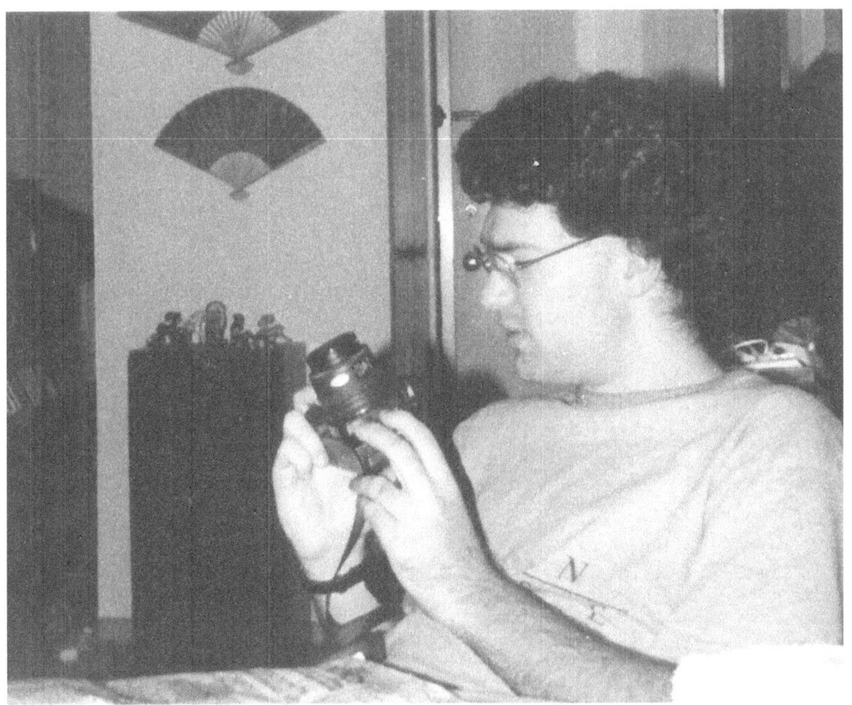

Life is meant to be shared.

Thank you to Christine and Colleen for their
proofreading and encouragement.

Thanks to
AAW: my feigned clueless blonde deity with the whopping
great key. If only he'd grown a beard at 18 or 20; my life
would have been so much simpler and happier.

ɕ

GRO: absence makes the heart forget; but this wasn't
acceptable so he tracked me down one last time to rip open
my scar tissue, pour acid on the fresh wounds, then smear
in super resistant bacteria to prevent any possible re-healing.
Even now he believes he knows better than I do how I should
interpret my own experience and what I should feel.

ɕ

DW: who followed me absolutely everywhere, gave me a great
day in Buckingham Palace, promised a lot and then didn't even
remember me when I went to see his play at the Duke of York. For
him I jumped off a cliff while blindfolded and ended up lasagne
spread over the jagged razor sharp rocks of the gorge's bottom.

1988

I WAS IN A 2 BY 5 meter dorm room in a five-story brick box on a Friday afternoon feeling free and adventurous but also a bit bored. It was late August, and my randomly assigned roommate had made it clear on the first day she had no interest in spending more time with me than absolutely required by the living quarters. So I'd gone to find the two people on campus I knew from high school. Sitting on the bottom bunk, I was waiting for them to return from their communal bathroom so we could go test my "fake" ID. It wasn't actually; it was genuine, just not mine, and had been generously handed to me on my second day on campus by an older girl who lived down the hall from me. She didn't look a great deal like me, but; for a bouncer carding 20 people in a go, I figured it was close enough. My friends were my high school prom date who asked me out of pity when no one else did, and my theatre buddy who was not so much any sort of an actor although pretty consistently a huge drama queen.

The door opened and in they came. Dom and Randy had brought along some others from their floor but I didn't clock anyone else at all aside from the guy that seemed to be glowing warm bright gold. Not exactly a halo but all around him there was – to me – a visible aura and it was entrancing. Elated at the sight of him; someone I'd never laid eyes on before, utter happiness filled me. I nearly bounced in place on the mattress but caught myself. His name was David, and from that second, I first glimpsed him; he owned me. I bowed my head trying to avoid being completely obvious. His angular but lanky build towered over the lower bunk, blue eyes under dark black hair, and I had to think to remember how to breathe so I could utter a hello and say "my name is Cherie". It was gratifying he was NOT wearing the typical uniform of jeans, sneakers, t-shirt, and baseball cap. That might've significantly changed the course of my university days if I'd managed to shake free of the spell through revulsion at his attire, but he was in a proper shirt and wearing real shoes.

I've since thought back on that moment often, wondering if he mightn't have had on some pheromone concoction making him irresistible like the boy with no own scent in PERFUME; or Matt Damon's character in the OCEAN's movies if that is an easier reference for you. Just being physically near David was heady to me, but no one else seemed affected. My senses would heighten, and I'd feel a charge but also peace and calm at the same time (the latter sensations not too familiar to me at seventeen). I imagine addicts feel a similar thrall on taking heroine. Whatever it was that he had to take me in with before even uttering a word, I don't know. He smiled at me, and I was captivated. It took everything in me to keep a cool head and play it down. Not sure whether I ever truly entirely pulled that off, but I tried with every fiber of my being. David said I reminded him of Debbie Harry and that was a tad disconcerting given she was born on the same day as my mother (i.e.: 25 years older than me) but I took it that he meant it in a nice way. I'd made an effort and had put blue and red streaks in my hair for my first night out on campus.

The group of us went out to a pseudo-Irish bar where none of us were caught out for being underage. Later I learned we were only a handful because a lot of the guys on Dom and Randy's floor were teetotallers. Ha. That lasted about a week. By the end of the first semester, there was only one guy that wasn't coming out with us, and he flunked out anyway due to lack of brains rather than having numbed them like the rest of us. Anyway, that first night with the guys was the first time I'd been able to relax and be myself since I'd done my sophomore year in boarding school (that incidentally was cut short as my enjoyment of it didn't serve the punishment aspect intended when I was sent there). He told a funny story about how his parents had sent him to a survivalist camp, and he'd been expelled from it for breaking into the kitchen at night to get extra food rations. I opened up, and we talked about who we were, the music we listened to, the movies we watched, the classes we were going to take, and with every exchange, I was more sure I'd met my person. At one point out of the blue David blurted out I was a rare beauty because of my green eyes and did I know only 2% of people have them? He was pretentious but felt genuine. He lacked a lot of general knowledge but that didn't diminish his attractiveness. He'd grown up with two personas: one for his middle class educated father's family and a different one for his trailer park mother's. This is what drove him to pursue acting. He felt detached from the things that ran the lives of others but he'd learned to mimic to fit in. I connected with that as I'd spent my life feeling like a bird being raised by fish. My parents had issues and I'd been sent here and there among relatives as often as they were able to get away with. Everywhere I'd been, I felt suffocated by attitudes and rules I didn't identify with. I'd never been any one place long enough to make the sort of fast childhood friends other people seemed to take for granted.

At the end of the night, David walked me to my dorm and then we were kissing under the trees. I don't remember the moment it started only that we were suddenly kissing, probably because it took me unawares. I'd only ever kissed three boys up to that point and it had really only been experimenting. I hadn't felt anything for the boys I'd practised on. But when David pinned me against the trunk of a tree holding my wrists by my waist I felt my breath leave me and something flashed inside my brain. I was abruptly entirely sober. He was much stronger than he looked, maybe because he was so tall – about 6'2" – and it was a good thing he pressed up against me because I felt myself dissolving. My knees actually wobbled a moment.

A stasis bubble seemed to form around us while we were under that tree because it seemed brief to me but at the same time each millisecond extended and burnt itself in my brain. I went inside after he'd gone toward his own dorm; after a large group of rowdy girls that stood too nearby for too long broke the mood, and on my watch 40 minutes were missing. No idea how that happened. I also don't know how I got upstairs to my room but I was there when suddenly I realised I was cold. I'd been out all night without a jacket. The next day I had a 101° fever. My roommate Jessica ordered me not to breathe in her direction because she didn't want to get whatever disease I'd brought into our unwillingly shared space. The campus health service was not helpful until the Monday when they gave me antibiotics for a bronchial infection. Yay. When I next saw David walking across the quad he was nonchalant and dispassionate. It made me wonder until he said he couldn't remember how he'd gotten home that night. It took everything I had in me to hide how I was reeling that he didn't remember. I wondered where the night had ended in his mind, but took him at his word because he did give off a novice lightweight vibe when we were ordering at the bar.

My second week at university was not fantastic as I struggled through my classes, not so much because I was ill but because I couldn't concentrate. First I kept replaying in my mind the details of Friday evening's stasis bubble bliss. Then I had the chance encounter on the quad on a feedback loop in my mind analysing the way the sunlight had played on his hair, the way he shrugged his shoulders, the deep burgundy colour of his shirt and the soothing sound of his voice. I couldn't compare any of it to anyone else I'd known. It was like I'd been wishing for years for a person like this to materialise and he had and every frame in my vision was precious. The more I analysed every moment and aspect, the more I felt David was ideal.

Repetitive grinding skidding crunching sounds underneath the deep rasping of a straining engine that intermittently revs as it lurches full pelt round the curves on a narrow mountain edge road. The interior is black and what I can see of the hood from the back seat is black, nearly as much as the India ink sky. There are a few stars giving off just enough light for me to see the steep vertical drop from the window as I quickly glance down, then back again to the wheel that has no driver between it and me. I am inextricably tied into the back seat. I pull and tear at the binding keeping me in place but cannot make any headway against it. My fingernails are broken and bloody from the effort. I try again to wrench forward reaching out with my fingertips to try and get the wheel but; while I've managed to cut through my clothes and into my skin, I cannot strain far enough forward to get even within a handsbreadth from the wheel. I am not; however, wailing or crying; although, that is not to say I feel nothing. I simply know it is a waste of time and energy to give into helplessness. My mind is despair and frustration and anger all focused on how to break free from the back seat. There are no doorknobs, no lock controls, no lighter… no crash barrier either. The centrifugal force around the curves throws me further into the gashes from the straps and the top of my head knocks on the window hard enough to leave a bloody smear on it but not enough to break the glass. Looking to the opposite side I can see the mountain is uneven, sharp-looking rock devoid of any plants. Suddenly the engine revs again as the climb becomes steep enough that I can no longer see the curve of road ahead and then the sound of chomping gravel ceases. I realise the car has left the road behind and is plummeting down when I get a weightless feeling in my stomach pretty similar to what you feel when a rollercoaster is just rising over the top of the highest rail. I am relieved and I sigh because this means I finally get to die. As I fall into the pitch darkness it is finally over and all of me relaxes for the first time since I can remember.

Here's where I get to brag. My time at university was pretty much a waste of money if the aim was to get a book centred education. It wasn't though. I was there to get a piece of paper so I could get a well-paid job and thus be free of my parents. I didn't even choose my major because my father did by electing the least offensive to him of the things I was willing to agree to endure. I sailed through all my classes and never had to open a book right to the end of my last year. I even finished in 3 years. My major was literature and every course required had syllabi filled with lists of things I'd already read at a younger age knocking around in libraries to avoid having to go home. In high school the AP English kids called me Ms Cliff Notes. When I hadn't already read it, I managed to glean enough from the in class discussions to get nothing less than 85% on any test or quiz. I honestly never opened a text book; save for personal entertainment or show, the whole time I was there.

All this was of course lost on David, who was trying to become an actor. Never mind that a university degree in acting does not mean you know how to act and puts you in a huge debt hole that most actors' salaries couldn't pay off in a lifetime. Never mind that apparently most of the people who were successful in movies at that time were either doing their own indie projects, or had a leg up, or were just dumb lucky. He would create things that I'd seen before or read somewhere else and he'd think he was being original. One day he was swaggering proud of an exercise where his classmate dressed as a punk and led him in leather skivvies around on a dog collar. They showed me a sketch of what they'd done to prepare. I didn't have the heart to tell him it was straight from an Almodovar movie from the early '80s. It didn't really seem to matter though as I was besotted and he had the kind of charisma that makes you appreciate the showmanship more than the substance. But anyway, my point is that despite a LOT of daydreaming and sleepless nights thinking about David and replaying every encounter instant by instant in my mind like the future of the universe depended on my being able to reproduce those moments; I was getting by in my classes. My performance didn't fail despite not really paying much attention to the objective for attendance at uni; except I did go to class so I might run into David on the way there or back.

David and I fell into a pattern in the first months of undergrad. I'd meander over to the guys' dorm on a Friday afternoon and an ever-larger group of us would go out. I was of course meeting up with Dom and Randy but I consistently homed in on David and if I was distracted by anything or caught up speaking with anyone else he seemed to find me. Other girls from my dorm floor; apart from roommate Jessica who was now in a sorority and was really only interested in frat boys anyway, started to come along when they realised this was a no pain way for them to start meeting males they didn't share classes with. We'd walk en masse to the same pseudo-Irish bar and soon the bouncers and bartenders knew us, so they stopped checking our IDs.

No matter the weather outside; the bar was always humid and warm from the throngs of people packed inside. There was limited space for moving around freely which suited the guys really well as they seemed to be religiously opposed to dancing. Once; going from the wall where we were standing across the space to the bathrooms, it was so packed that my shirt came unbuttoned as I pushed through the people with my drink elevated above heads. I didn't even notice until I was standing in front of the mirror and saw my shirt hanging loose on the sides of my bra because I had been so closely pressed against the whole time I was moving. That probably explained at least one smarmy grin I got while crossing the throng.

David and I and whoever was nearby would casually chat; as well as you can with loud rock music playing. We'd be sociable and sing along to the anthems being played. Anthems like American Pie by Don McLean that was from a generation before but had been played every night the bar was open since it had been released. Anthems like Led Zeppelin's Stairway to Heaven and STYX's Sail Away. This was not mainstream pop at the time; it was retro to when we had been toddlers at most. Did that say something about us that we rejected the music of our time? We preferred a music made by a previous generation that had abandoned their ideals to become the plastic hairsprayed brightly coloured money grubbers of the Reagan era. We didn't listen to Breathe or Spandau Ballet or any of that.

I became a passably good darts player. I'd drift in and out of all the conversations and did most of the introducing. At the end of pretty much every evening out like this everyone would wait until close and then people would drift into mini-groups for the 20 to 30-minute walk back to the dorms. My mini-group was always David and me. If someone else happened to try and join us, an excuse was made to drag it out so they'd get fed up and move along. We found nooks and crannies in the university buildings on the way that we'd disappear into. It seemed a little illicit in my mind because no one knew but us. I am not sure we were never seen, but surely by no one who knew us or there'd have been some commentary of some kind about us mashing on the way home, right? Mashing in my time meant kissing and maybe heavy petting. A far cry from what the Urban Dictionary says today, but that is how language evolves over the decades, I suppose. You cannot kiss someone in French without either offending them or getting their knickers off.

Eventually either I'd be shivering again, or nearby voices would rouse us or conversation would return and we'd get back to walking to the dorms. Every single time; when I saw David next it'd be as if nothing whatsoever had happened. You may think this is a poor reflection on my self-esteem that I'd let a man get away with treating me like that; however, while I never really knew what normal was I was sure it wasn't the life or relationships I'd had up to that point. None of my friends ever mentioned how their mothers were sedated or forcibly drugged by their fathers if voluntary sedation was refused. Given my mother was barely conscious during most of my formative years and my sister and I were like oil and water; my primary female role models growing up were what I saw on television.

To be honest, I was basically raised by popular TV since no one else was around long enough to make an impression or earn my respect. "Doctor Who" taught me ethics. "Cheers" taught me that the unremarkable can barely tolerate conversing with smarter or more educated people and that men admire philanderers. "M*A*S*H" reinforced both those ideas while also clarifying, via the fact that the doctors only conversed with the nurses when they were after sex, that whatever else a woman does, she is really only of value to an intelligent man if she's fuckworthy. I thought all those people in sitcoms were probably at least a reflection of what normal aspired to or what people out there in the wider world bought into.

"I DREAM of JEANNIE" taught me how to behave in a relationship. If you watch the episodes, it is unmistakable the astronaut is head over heels crazy about the genie; but the primary rule of their interplay is that to the rest of the world she must never reveal her existence. When anyone does happen upon her – usually via an act of trespassing in his private home, because she can only be taken out to places where no one he knows is likely to go – she's explained away as something other than the girl that lives with him and does his every bidding. Depending on the fiasco that is afoot it could be a granny, a male chef, a maid, a cousin, or once a mentally ill girl he's being benevolent with. The analogy doesn't stop there. Anything Jeannie may do or say that doesn't fit into the astronaut's notion of the world is dismissed as goofy nonsense that a real normal woman wouldn't displease her man with. Her relatives are all considered undesirable eccentrics and certainly never welcome. So to me that was a relationship of blind unconditional affection.

There is also truth in the fact that my twisted family life made me feel unworthy of interaction with apparently normal people. People who talked about how great their parents were, or how well they got along with their siblings or who generally seemed to feel ok with their lot in life rather than frustrated or cheated; were all like a different caste or culture that I could never belong to. When David wasn't with me I'd wonder why he'd want to be. His hands on me would make me forget that as desire overrode thinking. When he was being blasé and unemotional in the presence of any third party that came within earshot; I'd wonder if I was mentally ill and had just imagined all our intimate moments but I knew perfectly well they were genuine or at the very least fact. So I didn't know if I wasn't fuckable enough to go any further with, or just not good enough to be acknowledged. I'd go back into Jeannie mode anytime he was near and forget to care about reasons why.

Then the weekend before Halloween I happened to see David snuggling on the quad with a girl I didn't recognise but who looked vaguely familiar from the bar. It was pure chance that I'd left late and missed the group. After not finding them – unusually they'd gone somewhere different - I was walking back to my dorm alone on a route I didn't normally take because I'd looked around a few places to see if

I could find anyone. I didn't register at first what exactly I was seeing but David was obviously lip-locked with a girl I'd never had a proper look at. I tried to make myself see someone else but after standing there a minute and really seeing how oblivious they were to the world in plain view of anyone passing by, I realised I was not actually his girl. I told myself anything I felt was my own fault as he wasn't mine and he hadn't promised me anything whatsoever. In fact, when sober he'd never acknowledged any of what we did post drinks and so it was dubious whether he actually remembered any of it anyway. That helped me out on the logic that I was not allowed to feel sorry for myself, but didn't actually stop me from feeling sorry for myself. Or stupid and used and ugly and worthless. Obviously less desirable than whomever the fuck he'd been kissing on the quad; hand up her bra for the world to view and not hidden in the shadows, rather than wait for me to show up so he might've done that to me.

I didn't see David at all that week. I nearly ran into him on the quad but avoided him before he saw me. After a week of seeing in my mind's eye a continuous loop the images of David kissing the other girl, my aim was to forget who I was. On Halloween I went on a bender with Randy and Dom. The three of us seemed to be the only people on campus not dressed in costume. We went to two street parties before ending up passed out in a parking lot. We woke when a carrot and a ghost started shaking us to see if we were alive or dead. Come to think of it, it is pretty lucky no one parked over us or drove into us since we were just lying on the pavement. The carrot took us up to her apartment while the ghost made disapproving faces. I think she was interested in Dom believe it or not, despite his having been found by her in that state. We drank hoovers: two straws in one glass of extra strong daiquiri and first to the bottom wins… genius game for the cerebrally challenged. After that it was a blur again and I woke up in my own dorm bed with a taste of blood in my mouth and a note in my pocket -in writing I didn't recognise- saying 'don't be embarrassed'. Upshot is I indeed forgot my own name and most everything else that happened that night and was very unhappy that some mystery person thought I'd done something I might be embarrassed for that I didn't know about. I doubted I'd said anything revealing? I was lucky someone apparently took care of me though I'll never know who because Randy and Dom were also a blank.

When I sobered up on Sunday morning I still had all the pain of rejection and a sense of having been cheated on that I told myself wasn't justifiable since David had never said he was actually dating me or even acknowledged being involved with me in any special or particular manner (or at all). We had never discussed anything about our physical activities at any point. Even during them the most he'd say was "come here you" or "kiss me now" while he pulled me towards him. He sometimes would give cues of where we should sit or to alert if someone was coming by. The rest was all moans and breathing. I wondered if it were possible he actually didn't remember any of it. I felt connected to him by some kind of quantum entanglement but clearly he had no such feelings or he wouldn't have been kissing another girl. So my brain decided he didn't care about me but my heart wouldn't learn the lesson no matter how many times I revised and reviewed and analysed.

By late-November Sharon and Gail; who lived across the hall from me, were in openly acknowledged relationships with guys from Dom and Randy's dorm. Open as in people knew about it not the other meaning of open. Not sure if that means they were friends who hung out with me where I was or just girls who went where the boys were that I happened to introduce them to. Either way; while they never admitted to having seen anything directly between me and David, they did start to include in conversation that no one's opinion on anything seemed to matter to me aside from his. Thankfully this was in conversations with only females present; usually at meals in our dorm. They said they'd seen him eyeing me and why didn't I just ask him out? What was holding me back? Clearly I wasn't as stoic as I'd hoped because there was no question in their minds that I was attracted. I never confessed to them what had really been going on because it seemed that would be a violation of our privacy, but I did fancy the idea of being out in the open and not having to always hide. I wanted for David to acknowledge in front of another person the existence of whatever it was that we'd been doing; no matter what it actually was to him. I just wanted to have the peace of mind that it was at least important enough to him that he could remember it from one day to the next. Well, really no. I wanted to know for sure how he felt about me; which was clear as mud since he never expressed any feelings verbally only with his attitude, expressions, or physically. Over the course of a few successive meals of cottage cheese followed by puffed rice, I let Sharon and Gail plot how I should approach it.

There was going to be a special event where INXS was going to film something for MTV on campus and Gail; who worked in the student union ticket office, put two aside for me. The idea was to ask David to go as I knew he was mad for INXS and I also knew there was no chance in hell he'd get tickets on his own as that would mean having to skip classes. He would never do that. He'd never miss out on an opportunity to be the centre of attention in any dramatic exercise no matter how small. I got the tickets and had them in my pocket when I walked onto the guys' dorm floor late one afternoon heading to Dom and Randy's room. I was over the moon to hear David complaining to Randy that he hadn't known the forum was so small and by the time he'd gotten to the sales window there were no tickets left.

As I walked in I casually said "Oh, did you really want to go to that? I've got two tickets but no one to go with, but I don't think I'll go alone as that would be a bit weird." So David lit up and he said "Really, how much do you want for it?" Note the "it" is singular, making me think he meant the one I planned to give him anyway. I made a confused face and said "Oh no, I don't want your money. I couldn't ask you to pay." "Wow, are you sure? Where are they anyway?" "Right here" I said holding them up to show two centre seats. He took them both from my hand with a "Thanks Cherie. What a friend." He hugged me and I whispered "Glad to be of service," thinking this would sound cute and a teeny bit cool, but then he walked off around the corner and I just stood there while it listlessly emerged into my consciousness that he'd gone with both tickets and not said anything about how we would meet. I turned around and saw Randy on the other side of me looking miffed.

Randy said he knew my parents had money but what the hell was that giving away free concert tickets. I paused, tilted my head like a confused puppy, was about to open my mouth and then Randy said "He's got Becky in his room, he's been after a way to get her to go out with him for weeks and you've just handed it to him." "Who's Becky? I've never heard of her?" "She lives upstairs; she eats at our table in the cafeteria. When I asked her out earlier she said she wasn't interested in going to the bar with us because she was dead set on going to the INXS show… and not five minutes later I don't even have a chance at making a second try because David is going to take her and she'll forget about me by Saturday morning." I muttered "Oh, sorry Randy, I didn't know. No one's ever mentioned her; I guess I didn't think to ask?" So that's how Sharon and Gail's grand plan ended up going horribly wrong. I had never imagined the existence of a Becky. The idea David might have something on with whoever it was he'd made out with pre-Halloween had beleaguered my mind, but Randy never mentioned anything like a person regularly present and named. David had made out with me twice since Halloween anyway. Before committing to the tickets plan I had decided to think that quad kissing was a drink inspired one off. Now I had no clue what to think except that David took the opportunity I offered him to be with a different person. I wondered what Sharon and Gail would say about my having screwed up their generous efforts.

Randy barrelled on "Oh, sorry I didn't know. Well no, Cherie you didn't, I mean, what am I supposed to do keep you updated with bulletins? You're not around during the week Cherie." Dear reader, please remember this is 1988, before mobiles were commonplace, before Facebook updates to know who knew who and what they got up to, way way way before constant connectivity. Plus we lived in dorms that had one landline phone per room hung on the wall by the entrance door with a one-foot long cord. So if you wanted to talk to someone they had to be in and you had to stand practically in the hallway the whole time you were doing it. That meant phone chat was basically limited to making plans to meet each other unless you were happy to air all your business in public while the blood pooled in your feet. The exception to this rule was a girl named Antra who brought an 8-foot cord so she could talk long-distance to her boyfriend on the coast. No one else had that kind of drive or impetus to spend money on a long cord to enable private conversation from a bunk bed.

In other words, if you weren't familiar with someone's schedule and you wanted to be sure you'd meet up with them you had to plan ahead or you missed out. So I said, "Well, it's not my fault I don't live in your dorm Randy. You are my friend though. I mean who else am I going to talk to that will get where I am coming from? Aside from Dom I guess..." At that he snorted. He had little esteem for Dom and was basically only in the same room with him due to the idea that a bad roommate he knew would be better than a lottery with potentially worse results. Personally, Dom was a great guy. Dom was of a positive disposition and a little quirky; whereas, Randy was moody and malcontent. So we resolved from there we'd eat lunch together on campus Tuesdays and Thursdays. That way I'd know what was going on and not negatively impact his love life going forward. And I'd feel in the loop and yes, I'd bring other girls from my dorm with me, not just Sharon and Gail (who were unavailable but also not attractive enough for him).

After that we went to the bar and sang and drank with a bunch of other people but sans David who was with Becky at the INXS event. I chatted with a few more people than I would have otherwise. I waited until it was a decent hour to be able to go home without it looking like I'd scuttled off because I wasn't feeling right. A couple of the guys gave me flack for not staying to closing time, but then Gail made an excuse about being tired and wanting me to walk home with her. She felt sorry for me. When I got back to my top bunk I sobbed before I realised that she had actually followed me into my room. I had thought she'd gone into hers when I said goodnight. She asked me if there was anything I wanted but I mumbled I just wanted to be alone. I was grateful unfriendly roommate Jessica was now basically living at her boyfriend's apartment leaving me the room to myself.

Then Gail's boyfriend Jeff came across the hall — he'd followed about 5 minutes after we left — and came into my room as I hadn't locked the door (obviously given Gail was already there). I was lying prostrate with my head in my pillow. As they stood there their faces were right up by my pillow and only a hands width away. It seemed too close. While Gail and Sharon hadn't told Jeff who the guy was they had told him what happened. I think they were trying to protect me from humiliation. I wondered how long that would last as the story of a patsy giving two free tickets away might be gossip-worthy, independently of whether a frustrated attempt to ask a guy out was tied into the telling. But really I didn't focus on the humiliation for long as I had a dark void in the centre of my chest that was David not having chosen me or even considered at all going to the concert with me.

Jeff completely ignored what I considered convention refusing to give me privacy. He asked if I'd learned my lesson, a guy that would do this must be an asshole so clearly not the kind of guy I should be after. I kept saying "I know, you're right" in the hopes that he'd leave me alone so I might get back to my misery. He wasn't close enough to me to be giving me gratuitous advice. Gail barely was and we saw each other naked every day in the shower room. Jeff insisted if I had any self-esteem I would not pursue this any further. He was sick of seeing girls follow jerks around like fools letting themselves be walked all over – something about one of his sisters but I wasn't really listening because my brain kept echoing that David didn't choose me, didn't want me, didn't consider me when sober. So at some brief break in his monologue I said "Yes, I do have my pride; I will look elsewhere or not at all." With that he was finally satisfied and let me be. I was just tired and pissed off by then, unable to sleep. I just lay there awake wishing there were a TV in the room I could zone out with and trying to shut off the feedback loop of David hugging me before he trounced off with the tickets for fucking Becky. He'd said I was a friend. Christ almighty, if he were my just my friend we wouldn't have been making out. I couldn't even imagine anything bad happening to bloody Becky because I didn't know what she looked like. Argh.

After that I was treated with kid gloves by Sharon, Gail, Jeff, and an ever-increasing number of people who were told I had gone to pieces because I guy I had a crush on was oblivious. Thank the almighty IS that it wasn't ever mentioned who said guy was; or at least people didn't let on if they did know. They didn't know what really happened because I never told anyone about what David and I had been doing, precisely because my pride couldn't bear that much greater -in my mind- humiliation. So everyone just thought I was exaggeratedly fragile; and I was never able to mention any male again without them looking at each other worriedly.

Then the Christmas break came and went. I don't remember much of it other than my parents arguing and yelling at me that I was spoiled and not grateful enough for the presents they gave me. Thing is the presents they gave me obviously weren't for me but for some imagined substitute they would've rather had in the house. The clothes were a cut and colour I'd never have worn not to mention about 4 sizes too big. A cassette tape was of a band I'd never heard of and when I did try to listen it was poorly interpreted country music: pretty much the only genre at all that I have never liked, never feigned liking, and still don't like. Even the food my mother prepared seemed specifically chosen to show I was not even a passing thought for them. She served things I was and am allergic to, interspersed with things I've consistently refused for years because I didn't and don't like them. The hours passed with us sat in front of the tv silently except for the occasionally yelled order from my dad to get this or bring that or sometimes a casual insult or another manner of derisive put down.

Over the three weeks off I didn't manage to see Randy or Dom at all. Friends from high school were unreachable; which is not surprising since we hadn't spoken really at all in over four months. At New Year's Eve I was at home and went to bed at 12:01 because I couldn't stand to sit in boredom with my parents any longer than that. Dick Clark just wasn't entertaining enough to make it last to 12:02. I'd have preferred the MTV party, but that wasn't approved of, and we only had the one tv so fuck me. I tried to spend some of the last week reading in my room but that was taken as a personal affront by my father. He came in to rip the books out of my hands before ripping them into pieces while screaming at me to go and sit in front of the tv. Ahhh, homelife.

The first car cash I walked away from happened only a few months after I got my license. High school had just ended, and midway through June, I was turning left on a residential road when a car came barrelling down over the hill at least 40mph in excess of the speed limit. The front right of my car (passenger side) was hit by the front left of another car, and a crazed housewife bounced out of a damaged red compact shrieking that she was late enough already without this added grief. When the police came they didn't even talk to me. They took my license and stapled it to a report and turned to talk to the crazy lady. By the time the tow truck came I had withdrawn from being ignored.

When I got home my father didn't ask me what had happened as he'd already read the police report. The first person to listen to what I had to say was the insurance agent who called to get my testimony before settling; then changed his mind when he heard my side. Of course, the fact that the insurance agent did listen to me pissed my father off to no end. I was the heightened focus and special outlet of his inferiority complex for weeks after.

The day after the damage to my car was fixed I went shopping at the local mall. When I came out someone had banged into the same front right panel. I got that fixed out of pocket as my father said the insurance would cancel the policy if we claimed again so soon. Not sure whether that was true but anyway… The second repair lasted four days before someone in the local cinema parking lot kicked the same panel in. There was a converse footprint in dust right in the centre of the dent. After that I left it as it was and just drove around in a vandalised car until I had to sell it to pay for books, clothes and stuff to kit out my university dorm room with.

On return to campus after Christmas break, the start of the new semester was awkward because I wanted to avoid David, but I couldn't as Randy brought him along to lunch oblivious to my concert tickets humiliation. I couldn't say not to bring him along without giving myself away, so I smiled and faked that I was just as happy to see and chat with him as with any other person. I ignored that he insulted the girls that sat with me, and pretended not to hear when he whispered to me that Sharon ought to wear a bag over her head because the sight of her was nauseating.

I did manage to minimise my exposure to David via convincing Gail and Sharon that we should broaden our horizons by going different places and not always the Irish bar. So we went to a dance club one week. That would have been fun if I hadn't thought all the guys coming on to me were repulsive. They were far too slick and forward considering how little of interest they actually had to express. Also, Gail said my dancing was too provocative. Sharon said I was making them look bad so I ended up sitting at a table by myself most of the night when I wasn't asking berks to leave me be. The next week we drove to a Violent Femmes concert in another town and that was pretty fabulous as I'd never been in a mosh pit before. I LOVED the out of control feeling of knocking around en masse. Unfortunately, Gail and Sharon didn't like that at ALL so the week after we went back to the dance club again. That second time I just mimicked Gail & Sharon's moves and it was a bit boring but at least it was David free.

I finally found an outlet for my frustration toward the end of January when David sat down to lunch with one of each of the entrees. He picked at them and left most of it on his tray. This will sound like an austere old biddy but I've always hated when people waste food for no reason. It is probably my grandmother's influence because she lived through the depression and even after my father's family was poor. Any kind of food waste was considered the most egregious of all possible offences in our house. When other people throw mouldy items from their fridges I wonder how is it possible they didn't plan what they were going to eat. Even in movies; like the food fight in <u>Animal House</u> or the bulimic lawyer in <u>Legal Eagles</u>, I fast forward when I can't stand to see all that waste. Anyway, seeing four plates of barely touched food on David's tray, even if it was disgusting cafeteria garbage that I would never willingly put on my own tray, ticked me off. I asked him "how can you just waste that with all the people in the world that don't get enough?" He laughed at me "wow, you sound just like my mother". Great. Then he said it was Randy's fault. Randy immediately agreed it was his fault; because everything that was wrong in the world was somehow tied back to something he had done and he knew the first step to resolving things was to take responsibility.

I didn't know what ticked me off more now so I got up with a "whatever" and was about to go when I heard a thud under the table and then Randy winced and pulled on my arm. "Wait" he said "there's a party later at the Red House. You should come." I asked what the Red House was, was it a club I hadn't heard of? Turned out it was actually a house that was red that a bunch of people who had lived in their dorm the previous year now rented and they had a large back yard for a kegger. Sharon was sitting next to me so I looked at her and she said "why not Cherie? Let's widen our horizons." Note: the people at the table knew I didn't have pretty much anything to do on a Saturday so no excuses. So in my mind I was swearing like a sailor but I sat down and smiled so we could hash out where this place was and when we should be there.

After dinner I changed five times then did my makeup. When I saw myself in the bathroom mirror I had to change again because my face looked round and my dress - that on a flat girl would have looked fine - on me over my DD looked like a potato sack. Settling for something that made me look passable but was unfortunately not alluring; I wore tights with a suit jacket that closed at the waist. It was a waste of time really. In the second week of January it was cold enough that at an outdoor party no one was likely to take their coat off but I couldn't leave if I didn't feel like I looked right. Gail, Sharon and Antra were bored by the time I was satisfied it was ok to go to the damned Red House. Then Antra; who had broken up with her long-distance boyfriend over the break, saw me and decided she needed to change as she hadn't dressed up enough and she didn't want the guys to think she was just another buddy. For her the change was from black jeans to black pants. I suppose there must have been something special in the designs or the label or maybe the stitching, but all I saw was a not-skirt that was black. So we were later still than we'd said we'd be.

When we got there, there were already over a hundred people milling around. When my friends went to find their boyfriends I found myself standing alone by the keg thinking I should've brought my own bottle of alcohol because I hated beer. Arms surrounded my waist from behind and David hugged my back as he rested his chin on my shoulder. He whispered in my ear "hi there little girl." The blood drained away from my face and exited my entire body although I've no idea where it went. I tried to breathe but I made a pathetic sound like a whiny wannabe indignant grunt, instantly angry with myself for not having keep silent. Looking up to the sky I saw there were stars out and tried to centre myself but he said "I've been waiting for you". My pulse sped up as he turned me around. David told me he wanted me to meet a friend of his that was down for the weekend and introduced Lara, who was standing next to him. It was the person I'd seen him lock lipped with on the Quad before Halloween. So he was seeing a Lara and a Becky?

Lara, to me, honestly, looked more like a boy than a girl now that I could see her full body not wrapped and entwined around David's torso. Lara was wearing a plain white t-shirt which looked like a fruit-of-theloom undershirt, and K-Mart jeans. She was short flat and dumpy with plain bobbed hair the colour of mouse droppings. Actually she looked like she might not be of age. That this person in front of me was a friend he'd have visit and grope outdoors threw me given how catty he was about how other girls looked. I asked her if it was Lara like from <u>Doctor Zhivago</u>; and she didn't know what I was talking about. When I explained she said she'd never seen the movie or even heard of the story. I found that hard to believe but when she asked me what it was about I started to tell her; then stopped short when I realised she wasn't paying attention.

Lara asked me where I'd gotten my coat so I told her it was the uniform at my boarding school. This was perplexingly interesting to her given her own clothes. She made a fuss about how much it stood out so I catchphrased "life is a gift so I wrap myself well". That scored zero impact on her face. Then Lara yammered on about how weird it was to be at a college party in such a rundown house. For me small talk has always been extremely uncomfortable as it feels a waste of time and this felt like small talk since it seemed she didn't respond to anything I said from my side but just sort of blathered randomly. Small talk now; after David had hugged me and whispered in my ear, after a month of avoiding him and that, after not seeing him over the Christmas break, this was just plain perturbing. I'd not been inside so I just kept saying "uhuh", "yeah", "hmmm" until she gave David an odd look just as I spotted Dom and abruptly left them saying it was urgent I give him the whatsamathingy he'd been adamant I must absolutely not forget to bring for him.

Less than a second later I'd linked arms with Dom and was leading him in the opposite direction to the edge of the garden where the people thinned out. Dom asked what I thought of Becky because he thought she was full of it. I said I'd never met her and he replied he'd just seen me talking to her, standing next to David: look there she is the one in the white t-shirt and jeans in fucking January. Dom thought it was a ploy to get some schmuck to give her his jacket. Probably David really since they were pretty much going out but maybe someone else to make him jealous because she was a game player.

There was no clear way to understand or believe it. David had lied about who she was and stood there watching us exchange stupidities until I escaped. I'd thought he looked content while we were standing there but maybe he was simply smug. What was he trying to do? She'd lied right along with him, so it must be some joke or prank they were playing on me in concert. A scream nearly escaped my throat but I managed to keep it together. Dom just stood there looking at my face, and then he said "If I'd known I would've told you to stay away from him. He's a bastard. He's not worth it. And she's a very jealous one indeed." Dom suggested we leave the party, and I was grateful for it.

Dom and I went to a diner where they served pie and coffee 24/7 and we sat in a corner booth. The waitress came by and we ordered chocolate coconut cream to split. Then I was forced to make some kind of explanation for the face he'd seen me making so I asked him to keep it in confidence (I believed he would as he was a good friend) that I had a massive[3] crush and I'd been led to believe David was interested but clearly not. I put it down to my own inexperience. I supposed I hadn't consumed enough romance novels to really understand how people are supposed to behave and I must be expecting too much.

Dom said this was all a load of bullshit. According to him guys have the same feelings girls do they're simply less articulate about it as a norm: John Cusack being a huge exception meant to prove the rule. I didn't know whether to agree with him or not but if it were true that maybe guys just don't know how to express themselves then wasn't it possible David was simply going about it the wrong way? Maybe this episode with Lara was an exercise for one of his acting classes; as he'd mentioned once they have to be the characters and make others believe. Dom wryly condescended that Becky wasn't an acting major but sure, it was within possibility that she was taking an acting class. He didn't know her schedule. He avoided her because he thought she was a bitch. He'd decided that one day she made a massive fuss about his clothes. Apparently, she was practically poverty line poor so anyone that can afford more than bargain basement is a privileged prick to her. This for him, meant she was shallow and unable to see outside her limited sphere of experience. It satisfied me she was disliked by someone as considerate, congenial and likeable as Dom.

Then Dom changed the subject to his theory that WW1 was a classist plot hatched between the rulers of various countries to reduce numbers in the working classes because there was fear that with education they would overcome the system and the privileged would lose their proportional advantages. Looking back on that it wasn't very different from the underlying plotlines in the first three episodes of Star

Wars: masses of people being manipulated into devastating war by a few self-interested psychopaths. In the context of real history it seemed too over the top to be credible. Still, he made a convincing argument. The Black Tuesday Great Crash was also apparently driven by the top percentile of the wealthy elites because they didn't like having to share their exclusive rendezvous locations with people who'd learned to play the market. The waitress came with our pie apologising for having taken so long – she'd been waylaid by a troupe of drunken students ordering doughnuts to take away from the counter - and we realised 45 minutes had gone by since we'd ordered.

Post pie, it was 11:30 pm, and I was tired of sitting still. Having eaten overly sweet chocolate coconut cream, I figured my arteries could use some alcohol to counter the negative impact of the cream ingested. I said I'd read an article that confirmed alcohol in the bloodstream breaks up the fat so reduces the risk of hardened blocked arteries as you get older (wink wink). Dom now realised he didn't have his keys so wanted to go back to the party to get Randy's. So we went back to the Red House rather than any of the other at least a hundred places on campus we could've gone to get a drink. As we approached, I had butterflies in my stomach. Dom asked me a couple times if I thought I'd be ok and I said sure of course; could he stop asking already? I told him he seemed more upset about this Becky than I was. I wasn't ok though. As we approached the yard I realised that the crowd had thinned out considerably in the hour or so we'd been gone. David was immediately conspicuous as he was just now standing alone. Dom sighed and said he'd see me later but my eyes were already diverted as I replied "ok," and I didn't actually see where Dom went.

As my emotional magnetic charge forced me to walk toward David; Sharon and Antra blocked my path. Gail and Jeff had gone back to her dorm room and asked Sharon to give them at least two hours. Sharon was bored with the Red House and Antra didn't want to stay if Sharon left. I had made enough confessions for one night when I spoke with Dom so didn't want to argue too strongly for any path lest I give myself away, nonetheless did say I was hankering for one more drink. Antra had a friend in a sorority that had told her about a party at a frat where we'd get in because we were 'fresh meat'. I rolled my eyes but asked which frat and do you think we look bimbo-y enough to count as 'fresh meat'? David appeared at my right saying yes, absolutely we did, but were we going to leave him alone at this now dead party? "Well," I said perhaps overly wry in tone "we could get Dom, Randy and the others and go somewhere else." Antra pouted and shifted her weight so it looked like a stomp. David said Randy and the others had left a while ago. "Oh, but then we need to find Dom because he doesn't have his keys; he was looking for Randy." I started puzzling why David was hanging around apparently alone at this party. Had he come up to us because there was no one else around? Had he not thought to speak with Sharon and Antra until he saw them talking to me? What was going on and what was he really thinking? Was there any dimly remote possibility he'd waited around on the off chance I'd be back? I asked "Where's your friend Lara? Or Becky? What's her name?"

David looked smug to me this time. With a raised eyebrow he said Becky had left with someone else a while ago. That was it. No detail as to with whom or where to or why… I realised I was awkwardly studying his face when Dom came back and pushed my shoulder to snap me out of it. Dom was now stuck either going back to his dorm and waiting in front of his locked room door until who knew what hour or maybe we could all find something to do. We decided to just go to a coffee shop that was on the way back toward our dorms. The five of us walked there together but then David said he wasn't in the mood to sit under bright lights and left, purportedly to find something less garish to occupy his time.

After waiting half an hour to get served Antra and Dom seemed to be hitting it off but I was now inexplicably fatigued and not really thirsty anymore anyway. I asked Sharon if she wanted to go back to the dorm with me but she said "tic toc; I need to wait at least another hour". I offered for her to sit in my room as I'd be alone since Jessica hadn't come by the dorm at all for nearly a month now, but Sharon had ordered food so preferred waiting where she was.

So I walked back by myself. This was actually not a safe thing to do given that on campus on weekend nights in the wee hours there had been rapes of randomly chosen girls that fit no profile; but I didn't think of that at all. I was oblivious to all the people that crossed my path and was essentially on autopilot as I walked at an ever faster pace given I didn't have to wait for anyone.

On the way I was replaying in my head how David had come at me from behind, spinned me around and then the look on his face when he said we looked like bimbos. But then I'd remember Becky, and them standing there playing some game, and shake my head. It was infuriating that I could be so happy to see him – so breathless at the thought of his having briefly put his hand on my waist – while the whole time he was apparently having a private joke with fucking unremarkable pre-pubescent boy looking Becky. This looped a few times in my brain, and I was in the middle of shaking my head looking at the ground as I approached the steps to the front entrance of my dorm. Mid shake I saw in my peripheral vision that David was sitting there on a bench in the alcove. I stopped and looked down then looked back over to him. He was just sitting there bemused looking back at me. When I was sure it wasn't my imagination; which took a moment, I felt a pull that made me approach and ask him in a surprised whisper "what are you doing here?" "Waiting for you silly" and he reached up to grab my arms and pull me down next to him.

My first thought was that someone might have seen him there and that was a risk wasn't it? But he'd waited for me right? What did he really want and did I care so long as he was here now? David looked at my chest then raised his eyes and said "Cherie, I've missed you" and was about to kiss me when I pushed his shoulder away asking "what about Becky?" He grinned "don't you worry about Becky. Come here you" and he kissed me and all my muscles relaxed suddenly and I realised how tense I'd been and that it had been weeks since I'd felt the least bit unruffled. I disintegrated as a moan escaped. He pulled back then, grinning again, saying I should try to keep it down. I shifted back into Jeannie mode and suggested we could go to my room for privacy since

I had it to myself. He raised an eyebrow but we went in and up without coming across anyone. It was too early for most of the drinking crowds to be back and too late for people who'd not gone out. As we went up at first I was self-conscious because he was palpably eying me up and down. Then he put one hand on my lower back and the other on my arm and it seemed we were inside my door in a blink. As I turned to lock it and put the chain on he pushed my hair up from the back of my neck and kissed it while his other hand wrapped around my torso.

David turned me around again and pushed me against the door and kept kissing me as he unbuttoned my coat, then my jacket, then my shirt; only pulling back to locate buttons, and finally he put his hand over my bra. I was short of breath and a bit giddy when he came out with "Hmm, red lace… you slut" at which I cringed and he said "oh no, no I didn't mean it that way. Shh." He drew me against him, kissed my neck and then hugged me. He asked which bunk was mine. I said the top one but not to worry it was reinforced and had a wooden plank between the mattress and the frame. I was thinking about the weight of two people on it. He was jovial again so I inferred he must've thought I'd meant possible noise from the springs. As I climbed up the ladder he held onto the bottom of my coat so I was forced to take my arms out of the sleeves and my jacket and shirt went with it like layers of onion paper. I ended up without anything but my bra and tights by the time I was up top. He took his coat off and climbed up the ladder; leaning over me as he came over the top. I was sitting up and scooting backward until he grabbed my shoulder and told me to stop being squirrely and lie down. That made sense given the bed was a single.

Then he was leaning over me, kissing over my bra as one hand moved down over my gut to between my tights. I wasn't worried about what might happen or who might hear but I was anxious I might disappoint. I whispered "wait, I…" wanted to say I'm a virgin but he put his free hand over my mouth and said "shh, no more talking". By now he'd somehow unbuckled his belt and unbuttoned his pants and I realised he must've done it as he was coming up the ladder because his hands had been on me since he got up. "But wait, I" and his hand was over my mouth again. He was smiling saying "I'm not going to hurt you, just trust me" so I shut up as best I could given what his hand was doing in the triangle between my legs, and decided to trust him.

A short while later; when he'd gotten my tights down and off and my panties off he kneeled between my legs, spread them, and took a long look as I lay there watching his face. I adored him. I know it is cliché to say you adore someone. With overuse, it's lost its meaning but I felt peaceful divine bliss watching him look at me and looking up and down every part of me. Then he leaned over and seemed to be rubbing his penis everywhere between my thighs but without actually going in. I had a strange thought about a wildlife doc where animals marked their territory and clearly I made a quizzical face because he whispered in my ear "I'm crazy about you sweetie". Then he was abruptly inside me and colossal pain surged as quickly as I gasped. David stopped for a moment and said "you're a virgin?" I nodded and was petrified he'd be displeased or disenchanted but he just said "well, it's too late now" and carried on. I played with the hair on the back of his neck and ran my other hand down his shoulder. Afterward he bit my nose and kissed me on the cheek.

Then we just lay there. I was probably a tiny bit shell shocked because nothing was running through my mind. I was simply watching David's face, and looking at the rest of him, too, let's face it. But I wasn't thinking about what it meant or any of the things that I'd wonder later as I was consumed by the physical feeling of him and the smell of him and the sound of his breathing and how attractive he was. I didn't stop to think about Becky because he'd said not to think about her. David was on his back next to me and he stretched his arm over the top of my body putting his hand over my crotch with some pressure. He sighed "this is mine now" and didn't let go until after I'd fallen asleep.

That's how I gave my virginity away in the wee hours of January 28th, 1989 at the age of 18.

On a sweltering 107°F day mid-August (42°C for the non-US readers), I was stuck in gridlock on the Eisenhower Expressway into Chicago. Four lanes across plus the exit ramps were all clogged with cars that reflected and magnified the sunlight. The road itself seemed like it was starting to melt from the heat, and a haze drifted up from it as I sat there in my out-dated throwback of a beater with no air conditioning and a radio with dial knobs on it. At first, I'd thought myself lucky to have had the foresight to bring along a bottle of water for the drive into town, but the water bottle had been sitting in the passenger seat for over two hours and was hot to the touch. To top it off my seats were black Naugahyde (a vinyl kind of plastic leather) that was sticking to my legs and the backs of my arms making it painful each time I tried to move as I'd have to peel my skin off slowly to avoid a band-aid type yanking, and think hard before putting my limb back near the seat. I had tried sitting on a cloth at some point but it slid around making me lose my footing on the pedals.

Having started the journey looking ready for an interview; that I was now late for because of the stopped traffic, the rearview mirror showed my makeup was a mess, and my hair was damp. Guessing there might be a broken down or overheated truck across lanes ahead somewhere from a radio report that was oddly not specific about which interstate that had happened on; I realised it would be a while yet before we moved. I used the paper with my printed maps and directions to fan down the neckline of my button-down blouse and then up from the waistline and then leaned forward to get between my legs, my neck and back. I could see people in the other cars around were not doing anything like this so supposed no air was nearly obsolete. Everybody else had windows rolled up and was singing to music, arguing with their kids or just looking bored. One guy a few cars down picked his nose and ate it, making my stomach turn so I looked around behind me and saw there was a man in pricy looking casual clothing getting out of a silver Jaguar two lanes over.

This man looked to be about 40, but despite his age, he wasn't too ugly. It unnerved me though when I realised he was walking over to my car. And then he was standing at my rolled down window and leaning in way too close. He said "I saw you from my car and haven't been able to stop thinking about how striking you are. It looks like this won't be moving for quite some time so I wondered how much you would want for a blow job?" I didn't register it and just sat there looking at him; then asked "what? Sorry I don't think I heard you." He said "How much for a blow job? You look marvellous. I've missed the date I was driving in for and I'd like to make the most of the trip in." I started to laugh "you're kidding right? If you're not kidding I don't understand why you think I'm a prostitute because I'm not. Really." "Oh, I'm sure you know how even if you've never charged before. Look at that mouth" and his hand moved toward me making me lean back away from it and hurting my arms that had gotten stuck on the seats again.

The rest of the expressway seemed to disappear as the only thing in my line of sight was this guy's leaning leering face and his hand that lingered outstretched. The doors were locked but he was now closer to the switch buttons than I was. "Please go away. I'm not interested." My voice was low and hoarse. He seemed to deliberate what he'd do then his hand retreated as he stood up straight. "There's nothing to worry about I've got tinted windows, see? You'll surely appreciate the temperature in there." "Leave me alone." I started to crank the window up but that meant I had to get close to the door, and he took advantage of that to put his hand on my shoulder, making my entire body shudder with an intense spasm of horror and revulsion. He pushed my shoulder, and his face was suddenly right up next to mine.

He looked nasty now. "No need to play the prude, I've got plenty of money so ask for what you want." "Please leave me alone and go away. You're pathetic if you have to pay for it and just fucking depraved if you think all women are whores." I regretted having said anything as he replied under his breath "you think I'm pathetic do you? I should take you to the back of my car right now." I started cranking again as fast as I could make it go and saw him decide whether to put his other hand in or take the one he had on me off. He did the latter then stood there glowering at the car. I heard him say "fucking stupid bitch" as he kicked in the side of my door just as I got the window up. Then I peeled myself off the seat and went around the other side and rolled that one up as fast as I could, but when I'd done it realised he was walking back to his own car so I rolled the passenger side one down again and kept an eye on it until the traffic started moving again.

I woke up shivering naked in bed with no covers and David gone. He'd apparently opened the window before leaving. I moved to get to the ladder. My head throbbed and my legs ached like I'd done a million lunges followed by a million squats. I supposed I had used muscles that had never been used before? Every step down was awkward but I did get the window closed and took my coat up to use as a blanket since going as far as the closet to find my actual blanket seemed far too much of an effort. It was pretty early on Saturday morning, so lying in with impunity was probable.

I replayed in my mind every millisecond of interest from the night before in slow motion a few times. No Becky bullshit now; just David David David. David waiting for me David in my room and David in my bed. I pretty much felt like Scarlett O'Hara the morning after Rhett has his way with her. I realised though that I had not an inkling whether I'd done anything right. My sex-ed was all about the biology; as in limited to what we'd seen in biology class that was essentially a couple of diagrams of human organs and 20 minutes of chat before moving on to dissect pigs and then quickly shift focus to plant stamens. I could count on one hand the number of R rated films I'd seen with sex in them. Remember dear reader this was before internet so I'd had no free access to porn growing up, no one ever messaged me photos of their privates, and people generally talked a lot less openly about these things than they did post the influence of Madonna's SEX and Sex In The City.

David's penis was actually the first penis I'd ever seen, and I had nothing whatsoever to compare it to that might make me think it was more or less anything at all than anyone else's penis. The films I'd seen had been on cable at friends' houses since we got carded when we tried to see R movies at the cinema and were eventually too embarrassed to keep trying. Even the most lewd or sexually detailed conversations I'd had up to that point were in the confessional when priests would pry to know whether I had impure thoughts or masturbated; which frankly I didn't because I wouldn't have known where to begin. All those explicit questions did was convince me that all priests are perverts; like I needed more reasons to stay away from the church aside from the sum of all logic and science. Anyway…

About 30 minutes before breakfast would be closed, Gail and Sharon knocked on my door and we all went down in pyjamas and robes (one of the luxuries of being in an all-female dorm). I asked Gail where was Jeff, and she lit up like a kid being served birthday cake. Jeff had gone to play tag football. We were then regaled with a 15-minute description of the team he played on, his position in it, their win-loss record, and how good he looked in his kit.

By the time she started to quiet down we were sitting with our trays in a booth. "Sooo," Sharon said with feigned coyness, "how does Jeff rank on the Gail performance scale then?" "SHARON!" Gail screeched, "What kind of a question is that? Jeff is more than that. This is nothing like the guys from high school." "Well, I suppose this is the longest you've ever waited before giving in." Sharon was grinning as she said "Besides, it isn't the first time you've said a guy wasn't like the others either. I'll bet he'll get a ranking eventually." As Gail saw the surprise on my face, embarrassment grew on hers. I cried "No! No no no. Gail I admire you. Please don't misunderstand my face. I'd love to have your help. I mean, if you don't mind, it would help me a lot not to know rankings obviously but to -you know- have some pointers maybe." Gail sat up straight and snorted. "Really," I said, "I mean you know I've got zero experience and would like to know what is it like? Is it like poetry, songs? What genre of songs?" Sharon laughed out loud and Gail relaxed.

Clearly my small town sheltered upbringing – only able to go out if driven by a parent and then only to places where we might be collected from and thus never really free or alone - was not what these girls had known. In movies kids went to wild parties or wasted hours on end free from parental prying just about anywhere but I'd never had that luxury. No one I knew had their own car or was ever lent a car to use. I'd gotten a car in my senior year, but my parents kept such tight control over my schedule it only served to go and come from very specific places and they frequently showed up to make sure I wasn't somewhere else. They checked on me at the cinemas, at pizza parlours, at the mall. It quickly got so bad no one wanted to come along with me so I ended up just using the car to go to school and back until I sold it.

I knew Sharon and Gail had gone to inner-city schools and had the freedom to go where they liked, but hadn't really contemplated what that meant until now when they started to talk about their – to me seemingly – vast sexual experience and exploits. They asked me if I was a virgin so I told them there was never really anyone in high school I'd been attracted to, but even if there had been I'd never have had much opportunity to go anywhere intimate with them. They looked at each other so I asked, "what?" Gail said the first time she had had a boys hand down the front of her pants had been in the back row of the bus home from school; which was also the first place she'd given a boy a handjob. Apparently if there were enough coats and backpacks to keep people at a distance and you knew how to be quiet, you could get away with quite a lot on a bus.

Sharon said her first time had been to get it out of the way, but she hadn't really liked the guy. It had been a sloppy quickie in the basement while her parents were upstairs and they were supposed to have been preparing a project for school. It was her second boyfriend she had really liked, and they'd been together for nearly two years. In that time they had plenty of time to experiment. "What do you mean exactly, experiment?" Sharon said they'd done all the positions from a handbook his brother had given him that had graphic photos (about 100 in all), they'd done the blindfolded food thing from 9 ½ Weeks, they'd tried it on a washing machine, that kind of stuff. "Oh." I was actually amazed she'd even managed to get a copy of an explicit book on sex as even the <u>Joy of Sex</u> was banned from our town library.

Gail was bemused watching my reactions and said "so Sharon what advice do you have for our virgin friend here?" I took stock that they hadn't missed a beat and weren't giving me a hard time about it. They were being open. "Golf balls" Sharon said. "Golf balls?" I asked. "Yes, if you want to enjoy it when the time comes you've got to get in shape. Get yourself a pair of golf balls." "What do I do with them?" "Put them inside you silly. You'll get the feel of them and it'll tone you up." I just sort of sat there stunned. I'd never heard of such a thing. Gail said "don't worry about that Cherie, maybe when you've actually got someone in mind you can think about it then. Sharon's just obsessed with putting foreign objects inside her." "I am not" Sharon protested. Gail snorted "uh, yes you are. Let me list a few? Aside from a dildo, a round hairbrush, a stress ball, peppermints and ice cubes. And that's just the stuff I know about." Sharon gushed "You know you can't feel an ice cube inside you?"

"Really?" I asked. "An ice cube? Why?" "For him, he can feel it." I looked at Gail and said "Wow. Have you done stuff like this? I mean, is it actually what everybody does?" Gail said no, she'd never had a really long term boyfriend so she'd never gone off the deep end like Sharon. She had done the blindfold thing though; but didn't like it because she was convinced someone other than the guy she was with had been in the room during that. That kind of thing was to be done only with people you really knew you could trust completely. I said "well surely you must trust these guys if you are letting them inside you?" They looked at each other again and then Gail said, "Sometimes a person just wants what she wants. But definitely if you trust him, it is much much better." When we went back to our rooms, I saw through the open door that Sharon indeed had a container of golf balls on her windowsill. I made a note I'd have to find out where they might be sold on campus and think about where to hide them.

I feel the dirt in my mouth and occasionally, I see a tombstone above my forehead, but try as I might to rise or move I can't. I convulse and ache but can't get up. I strain but am barely able to look left or right with my eyeballs. My joints ache as I try to move and I can hear people in the space behind me but am unable to see or identify anyone. My eyeballs struggle in their sockets, but the best I manage is a view of shadows over me. Trying to scream the whole time, I am barely able to force out a wheeze. Trying to shout at the top of my lungs I hear barely audible mumbling under the whispers that fill the space behind me. I drift into dark then drift back to this trapped confusion then back to darkness.

David hadn't gone out with everyone else on Saturday evening, and I couldn't very well track him down to find him. I couldn't ask too much without giving myself away so when a casual enquiry got a "dunno" from Randy and Dom I kept my mouth shut and changed the subject. I'd gone through Sunday in a confused daze and zoned out in front of the television in the common room. I don't even know what I watched. It was just an excuse not to have to speak with anyone. Monday I was physically moving about like a normal person following her schedule but mentally, I was still in bed on Saturday morning.

When I finally saw David at lunch Tuesday it was like a glass of water after days of walking in blistering heat; despite the fact that he played so cool an outside observer would have had zero idea we were anything other than casual platonic friends. Of course assuming this observer did not see under the table when David put his hand between my legs just as I was putting a forkful into my mouth. We were sat very close around the table so it was in fact unlikely anyone would have noticed David's stray hand unless they were right behind him observing the movement of his elbow.

He did it while he was looking across the table at Randy arguing about whether the cafeteria menu was worse this semester than last. He was actually saying to Randy he thought the meat was better somehow as the tips of his fingers stroked my crotch one by one while his hand slid between my pressed thighs, which is when I sputtered. I narrowly avoided choking when I gasped just as I was going to swallow. He turned to me and smiling said "what Cherie, you don't agree?" and I could see a twinkle in his eye just as his thumb pressed my button. Bewildered, unsure if I might be having a sensory hallucination, feeling utterly exposed and yet I was earnestly afraid my underwear would get wet. I stifled a shrieky shocked cry as I muttered "wouldn't really know" feeling sure the whole table must be seeing me blush; but then I realised they would probably interpret it as a side effect of my coughing.

I thought back to the conversation with Gail and Sharon and wondered if they'd forgotten to mention this among the litany of what inner city teenage couples do? I mustered some self-control and tried

REALLY hard to concentrate on what Sharon was saying on the other side of me. I was looking at her nodding and hoping she wasn't saying anything I'd be asked about later because I had no idea whatsoever what she was on about. I really did try to listen and I watched her mouth moving trying to make the sound coming out of it align to the movement and understand. But I had no chance.

My thought processes were shattered and wouldn't come together again. I was stunned on the one hand that David was doing this so to speak in broad daylight. I felt he was being a bit viscous with me given he'd disappeared the morning after and we hadn't actually spoken since. I mean I was sure after what we'd done (and certainly given what he was doing in that moment) he must have the same feelings as me but he had in fact vanished without so much as a note. But, I was also melting into his hand and really straining very hard - as intensely as my wits could muster - to not moan out loud or squirm or frankly rotate into him; which is what my fluttering heart wanted. It might've been a panic attack but I felt my heart throbbing while I then tried to concentrate on my breathing while his fingers moved up and down slowly but with purpose, and I realised my lower organs were throbbing much more fiercely than my heart.

In my mind's eye all I saw was David's hand over my clothes stroking an area of my body that no one but him had ever touched. I knew I was starting to breath a bit heavy so focused again on breathing as I couldn't think how to move his hand away without drawing the entire table's attention. Mixed into the physical and the raw panic I think I was also pissed off at the liberty he was taking. It was so David to do this on the quiet under the table pushing me to my limits but careful that no one might know.

I never put my own hands under the table while eating because I was taught it is bad manners to hide your hands. Elbows should always be flush with the tabletop or your commensurate meal companions might suspect you of holding a knife. Very Machiavellian or perhaps this just came from DUNE; but the whole group currently sitting with me had actually had a discussion about it at one point when we first started eating together. I was stuffed because if I did differently now they'd surely remark on it and I'd have to explain what I was doing with my hand.

Suddenly I blurted "David, you're being rude. Where are your hands?"

His hand paused. He arched an eyebrow. Then in a wry exasperated tone he said "Cherie, if I try and move my arm now I'll knock things over. Forget your damn silly rules." Damn, this was actually true and evident. Randy and Sharon exchanged a sort of 'she's so odd sometimes' look then carried on with the conversations like nothing happened. Given he wasn't taking his hand away and it was ever more of a challenge not to writhe right there in the chair I spread my legs a bit. This regrettably (or blissfully depending on your perspective and opinion; but at the time I was in anxious despair) gave his hand more room to move. I could see David smile as he recommenced and I only remembered to stifle the groan when it was halfway out but it did seem to me Sharon thought this meant I was disappointed in David's manners or reacting to something she had said rather than anything else. Could've been either I have no bloody clue. Didn't David realise that just being within a foot of him gave me an electric type rush? Him touching me made me short of breath. Surely he'd noticed, so he had to be aware he was pushing me over the edge touching me there? Let alone in such wideopen circumstances?

So when Sharon said "Cherie, are you coming or not?" I almost choked again. Then David leaned into the back of my head and under his breath whispered "yeah Cherie, are you coming or not?" That husky hot whisper in my ear that felt like he'd spoken from within my own brain. How did the other people at our table not hear this you ask? Especially as we were packed so closely together. Among the noise of hundreds of students laughing, shouting, eating, trays clanging, and metallic fire doors slamming as people walked in and out the better question would be how did we hear each other or how on earth did I hear him whisper to me. Or maybe they did hear but it was a comment typical of his everyday sense of humour so they didn't think twice? I don't know but it appeared these people; that I spent so much time with and should know my expressions better than anyone, did not cop on to anything unusual in my speech or face and certainly not to what was still happening under the table.

"I … I … Sorry Sharon. What was the question? I spaced out there thinking about an exam I have this afternoon." I said as I looked down.

"Honestly Cherie" Sharon was exasperated "I'm off to class are you coming or staying?" David squeezed with his whole hand palm perpendicular to my legs and my vision flashed again. He was holding my body in place with that grip.

I shakily breathed deep; hoping it looked like I was considering my answer, before saying "I'm going to sit here a while and do a last revision of my notes. Sorry Sharon."

"Ok, see you later". Sharon, Gail and most of the rest of the table left. David and Randy didn't though. Randy was still complaining about the food and how the selections were not only unhealthy but bad for his complexion because of their high fat and sugar content even in the food that wasn't fried. I thought if I knew how long he'd been going on about it I might know how long David had been caressing mercilessly but I really wasn't sure. Personally, Randy was ahead of his time on food habits. Probably could be considered a pioneer of the metrosexual movement if it were ever actually considered a movement. At the time though he was like an unintelligible droning bug noise that I wanted to go away so I could address David and what David was STILL doing. Then, like he read my mind David interrupted.

"Randy, don't mean to cut you off mid-rant but I do in fact need to cut you off as the clock is ticking and I too have something I need to finish preparing for this afternoon."

"Oh! Well! Let's just shut the progressive thinkers up and shuffle them along then, is that it?" Randy said with mock offense.

"Absolutely Mister sharp as a tac." David grinned while he made a sweeping motion with one outstretched hand. The other hand was still making my personal private bits feel shamefully exposed and helpless although he was just keeping them firmly in his grip now. Just now is when I took my free arm and leaning down as if to get my backpack went under the table to grab his wrist. I tried to tug his hand away but I might as well have been pulling at a one-tonne weight. Either David was much stronger than I'd imagined or I was pathetically weak.

"Bye Randy" I said as he turned away taking his tray with him.

David looked at me and whispered hoarsely. "Please tell me you're as turned on as I am." I relaxed my grip on his wrist.

I whispered back "David, I'm afraid to get up. I'm not sure if I'm visibly wet."

He smiled what seemed a genuinely pleased and warm smile. "Now I'm not sure if I'll be able to get up. Cherie I can't stand it. Do you really have an exam?"

"No, I just didn't want to have to get up. I'm serious. What are you thinking doing this here? Don't you think it's wrong?" I pleaded. "Please take your hand off so I can check whether I'm going to be a spectacle when I inevitably have to stand up to leave the cafeteria."

He leaned close. "Relax; you're fine. And you are soooo fine. Let's go back to your room. You don't actually have a class for hours do you? No one else is around this time of day are they?" I was taken aback by the thought he might know my schedule as well as I knew his. But certainly, it wouldn't be too hard to keep track of if a person was minimally intelligent so I decided that didn't mean anything. He probably knew everybody's schedule at least vaguely. But I wasn't actually sure about Gail and Antra's at this time of day.

"I don't know. I suppose not." He raked his fingers up so they all brushed over the button of my clitoris again, and I felt a surge of anxiety as my vagina throbbed. I still felt more than a bit despoiled but at the same time I thought if I didn't get him inside me asap, I might lose my mind. I answered "but if you want to do that at some point you're going to have to let go your grip or I won't be able to stand up. How does your wrist not hurt doing that from where you're sitting?"

He chortled and moved his hand away. "OK, I'm withdrawing but I plan to put my hand right back there as soon as we're inside your room, before I put something else there." As I got up from the table I looked down at my crotch and it was true that despite feeling like I was wet it didn't show. This was literally virgin territory for me; but I should have realised clearly not at all for him. David walked behind me as we went to put our trays away, then alongside me but not touching me as we walked back to my dorm.

We didn't speak the whole way. I didn't want to ask him where he'd been Saturday lest he think I was being invasive or distrustful or overly possessive. We just walked side by side. I wasn't sure what I could say that wouldn't sound cliché or clingy. You know how your ears hum after a loud concert or a night in a club near the speakers? My female parts were humming, but instead of the aftereffect, it was the anticipation. Although I honestly could feel him inside in flashes as we walked so maybe it was a sort of flesh memory. I glanced at him a few times during the seemingly infinitely long walk back to the dorm and caught him checking me out, but he quickly moved eyes front to look where we were going. The negative side of what I'd felt while in the cafeteria was completely forgotten. As soon as we were in the stairwell his hands were on my butt like he was petting my behind as we went up and the humming felt ever more urgent; like an amp that had been dialled up to eleven. He could do anything he liked to me wherever he liked from this point forward. I no longer had any will of my own apart from the fervent desire he not stop or let go.

As soon as we were inside he delivered on his promise and I had joy and utter happiness before I had ecstasy. Flashes of white crossed my vision and he lay on top of me while our breathing slowed down. I thought about something they'd said in one of my classes about white being the representation of death. No wonder virgin brides are supposed to wear white. He croaked into my ear "I know this is soon but I think I love you Cherie." No human could possibly feel more joy than I did at that moment. It meant his feelings were on a par with my own. But I didn't want to ruin the moment so I just kissed him again. Then we talked about random nonsense while we lay there looking at each other. About movies we might go see, about his next performance exercise, about the cartoons in the campus newspaper, about the pictures on my walls. During a lull, I said as offhandedly as I could "you know I missed you on Saturday." He grinned "you did, did you? Can't let that happen again."

Then he wanted to know why were my bed sheets different designs in black? To me this was a silly question because by now he should know I wasn't a flowery pattern or cotton candy pink type of girl; but there you go. I had believed back then he was observing me and learning me as well as I was him; but looking back there were always these signs that in his head I was just an odd sort of girl rather than a specific, well-defined individual with tastes that weren't cookie-cutter standard. At the time though, I was so entirely caught up in my feelings for him it was just a funny question to answer with a laugh. And laughing and laying there the physical fun naturally started all over again. We lost the afternoon but he didn't lose track of the hours. He checked his watch in time to make sure he didn't miss his performance slot and left well before the girls started coming back to the dorm for dinner.

After that we slid into a pattern where we were sleeping together Friday and Saturday nights but he was always up and out before anyone might notice him in the halls. He didn't by a longshot fall of the face of the earth. We were spending the afternoons together in my room twice a week and sometimes more if he came across me on the campus. He really did know my schedule come to think of it. Every time we were together the physical was only a part of what we did. Our conversations were long and deep and covering any and all subjects under the sun or moon. He was the most important person in my life, the one I spent the most time with, the only one I was genuinely totally honest with. Of all the people I'd known up to that point in my life he was the only one who'd shown genuine interest in my thoughts and opinions for their own worth rather than as a starting point for refutation or ridicule. He was the one person who really seemed to want to know me and was also the first person who I held nothing back with; freely letting him see in my thoughts and openly know my emotions. I felt we had a clear understanding of each other's feelings because he'd said he thought he loved me *after* we'd had sex rather than as a ploy to get me to do it.

My mother's station wagon's front axle broke while we were on a road trip with some friends of hers. We were entering the onramp for the expressway when there was a shudder and thud and the car would move no longer. It took twenty minutes to realise the car would not budge; then another twenty for me to walk back to the rest stop and call for a tow. It turned out the tow came from the same rest stop but not for another hour and a half as we weren't a priority accident. The mechanic took another half hour to decide the dark maroon station wagon with faux wood panelling on the outer doors couldn't be fixed right there on the onramp. FINALLY it was towed the 150 meters back to his shop. He said that for an axle to break the way it had was either down to intentional damage or really extremely long odds. We were lucky we weren't dead because if the car had been on the expressway when the axle broke for sure we'd have been in a dire accident. The odds were so long the mechanic didn't believe it could be anything other than intentional. We wondered silently whether perhaps someone had for some reason wanted to remove one of us from the face of the earth.

Silly, right? But then men murder their wives every day all over the world. If misogynists aren't murdering their women they are throwing acid in their faces to scar them for life, or raping them, or in some other way degrading them or making sure they understand their existence is thanks to being allowed to exist by a man who has power to make their lives difficult. Personally, much of the porn that circulates (admittedly my judgement is based on a small sample of stuff I was forced to watch post-grad for a study); when not so far gone it's illegal, is really mostly misogynistic. If the porn industry were driven by healthy desires for sex between equals there wouldn't be so much of it that reduces women to body parts or that requires submission. Misogynist porn certainly couldn't exist if it weren't for an extended silent populace of men consuming it, and a lot of not so silent ones too. Not that my wifebeating father was the type to consume porn; but he was certainly not beyond daily degradation and or humiliation aimed at nullifying my mother's personality. Most days she simply wasn't allowed to express anything; being shouted at to shut the fuck up if anything coming out of her hole seemed like it might distract him from his television programme or in some other way annoy him.

So no one said anything while we waited for parts to be brought in from the city and then for the car to be fixed. No one even cracked a joke about it. The repair literally took all day and no one even made light of what had happened. The waitresses at the diner looked like they felt sorry for us and offered us a round of free desserts but then got bored when they saw hours later we still hadn't moved on. The friend my mother had brought along avoided speaking about anything other than recipes during the full eight hours we spent making time while we waited and waited and waited. It was very late at night by the time we finally got back home.

My father's nonchalant reaction when we got home and he apparently didn't care that my mother could have died; or that for this type of thing to happen was not normal, upset her deeply. But her mention of divorce was as brief as it was empty. Aside from the fact that a smack across the jaw made her shut up and cower; she could never have left the situation she was in. She had absolutely no way of making her own money unless she started working for a fast food chain and even that probably would have been too difficult for her. Like so many other women of her age; she was tied to a man due to her inability to make her own living given she'd never finished school and had no other independent means. We didn't live in a state that gave a woman half and she knew she would have been lucky to get child support as her alleged mental health issues would probably mean custody would go to him.

However; women in her generation weren't raised to think this was a form of servitude or essentially prostitution; which is female service in exchange for money, as marriage then incorporated obligatory sex. She would tell anyone who asked she was a good housewife because she and a lot of women of her generation were more terrified of being alone and struggling to get by than of being prisoners in their own lives. Even now I know many women and men who live in stifling relationships with people they don't have good feelings about because it would be HARD to extricate themselves and make a life on their own. Economics and lifestyle still apparently weigh more for many people than happiness or love. Or maybe those people don't believe in love anymore anyway so what difference would it make to them if they lived alone? Or maybe they never believed in love and thought of marriage like a business arrangement of convenience. All speculation given most of those people I'm contemplating were never on their own. They went straight from parents home to collegiate shared living to marital dwelling.

Anyway, thirty years later I was going five miles an hour in rush hour traffic after work when my relatively new car shuddered then thudded then stopped. I looked around bewildered but was sure I hadn't hit anything. I tried moving forward then back then forward and all I did was make the clutch burn. I got out to see if there was something in the road but there wasn't. I called on my mobile phone for a tow and they said due to the time of day it might take two hours for one to get to me. This was despite me emphasising that I was on a one-way street obstructing the passage of said street. They said they'd notified the police to sort out any traffic violations. Thinking they hadn't understood but what could I do; I had to wait in the middle of traffic for the tow to come and I was alone in my car. The entire time I waited people whose paths home I was plainly blocking periodically came up to scream at me to get the god damned fuck out of the way. One, another, one more, then another, then another. Each time I would mime from inside the car that I had called a tow on my mobile but they would take so long to get there. Each time the reply was abuse hurled at me through the window before the person turned around and huffed of.

After 25 minutes a gang of 10 men came up to my window and told me they were moving me. With me still in the car; because frankly I felt like I was the centre of an angry mob and wasn't getting out no matter what, they attempted to push it. When they couldn't make it move forwards they tried moving it back. After 10 minutes of pushing back and forth and the car not moving even five centimetres a few of them started kicking the sides in. I, of course, stayed inside with the doors locked until the police came with their own tow because my tow was running late and they wanted to clear the road. The gang of men had made haste as soon as they saw the police coming close. I couldn't have identified them anyway so what was the point of filing anything regarding that? The genius who hooked the car up to the tow said of course the car couldn't move as the wheels were pointing opposite directions. My axle had split and he showed it to me; looking at me like I had suggested otherwise or was of less than average intelligence as I hadn't known to say this when calling the rescue service.

Due to the episode with my mother when I was 15; when my own axle broke on my own car 30 years later I was convinced at the very least it must be a factory defect. It couldn't possibly be normal wear and tear in a car that had only been on the road six months. I suppose the kicked in sides of the car didn't help my claim against the manufacturer. How would they know if the damage was before or after the axle broke? Did I get anywhere at all when I complained to the dealership, insurance or workshop? Of course not. I was a woman with no mechanical background dealing with a world of men used to dismissing a female opinion out of hand. In this case mansplaining would not have been a complaint from me, but their attitude really did piss me off. They all said I must have driven into a pothole and the axle showed a clean break so wasn't down to quality of the part. I had not, in fact, driven into anything but they asked me to prove that I had not driven repeatedly over potholes for six months. As if it were any more possible to prove a negative in driving history than in any other part of life or logic. I thought back to my mother and how, if the mechanic dealing with her had been that dismissive in his assessment, she could have saved herself a bruised face and probably some vexation wondering what had really caused the axle to snap.

Halfway through the semester it was a wonder people around us still hadn't copped on to what David and I were doing. Maybe they did and they just kept quiet? I don't think so, though. I don't think my circle of friends was really mature enough to complicity stay quiet out of respect for (or lack of interest in) my intimacy. They whooped up and down the halls about each other's pickups, and I don't see why they would have spared me from it. Sometimes watching them tease someone coming back to the dorm doing the walk of shame a morning after seemed like watching hyenas ripping into a vulnerable gazelle.

For me, it really was a double life. In front of others David and I were certainly chummy and friendly but not overly physical. It was hard sometimes not to talk at least to Randy to ask his opinion on something David had done or said. I had no references or input unless I spoke vaguely about obscure movies to get people's impressions of some of David's behaviour. EG: "I saw this movie once where the guy snuck into a girl's bedroom every night to sleep with her then snuck out every morning so no one in her family ever saw him. They only realised she was seeing someone when he slipped off the roof and broke his leg." Sharon would say "How did he slip?" "I don't remember… Maybe it was icy? Anyway, is that really plausible?? Do you know anyone that did that sort of thing?" "Sure, not all the time but now and again sure." This was pre-TWILIGHT. Nowadays it is probably part of every teen girl's fantasy or even expectations to get nightly nocturnal visits from her boyfriend. I suppose this conversation seems trite and childish, probing via third party fictional example whether one's own reality is normal. That was my reality though. Hearing her say "sure" made me feel ok, even though it also meant I'd continue hiding it from her and everyone else.

I also thought - at the time - the secrecy made things a bit exciting. I thought if David wasn't ready to be out in the open there must be a reason. I didn't want to pry into that because he could be strangely private about a lot of things. It was really part of his nature to keep things close to his chest; having grown up between social strata always hiding a part of his knowledge, tastes, experience or self. I felt I did the same thing. No way on earth was I going to speak with him or anyone about most of the nasty details of my own home life growing up; except in passing or generalizations. It suited me just as well that he not pry into things that made me feel inadequate as a human being let alone as a mate or girlfriend or partner or whatever he might think of me as. So; half way through the semester he was my closest friend but he only knew a part of me and I was fine with the idea that he only share what he wanted me to see because I believed no matter what there may be, it sure as hell couldn't be as bad as what I was hiding. In any case, isn't that part of what love is? Wanting to be better people for each other? So we wanted to be with each other who we really WANTED to be rather than drag around the negative baggage life hoisted on our youths. I think that made our connection more real and confirmed in a way we were mentally in sync. Still, we were treated by the people who knew us like two close friends who were both single but not attracted to each other. HA! Nothing farther from the truth (at least from my side) but there you go.

Just before Easter break David said he wanted me to go home with him to meet his cousins. I had told my parents I was staying at the dorms to study. The idea of a few days off-campus with my David seemed too good to be true; much better than a week alone on an empty campus. David said he wanted to see how I'd react to his family and how they all lived. I laughed, thinking that was an odd thing to say, but we did quickly plan a trip to the trailer park where his mother lived. My mistake was to mention it in the cafeteria thinking no one else was paying attention to our lunch line chat. I was just running my tray along the rails as I couldn't stomach anything I saw aside from the cereals and salad bar items; pretending I was giving the food at least some consideration. I asked what time should I be ready to go down to his car? Randy had snuck up behind me in a way only he was able to do. When David saw him David said it depended on when everyone else could be ready. He asked Randy what he was doing Friday.

After a brief explanation, Randy exclaimed, "What's this? An impetuous spring break road trip you say? I'm in." Damn. So I'd have to keep the facade around his family too. Well, it was still better than the prospect of a week alone and it was still so many stratospheres better than having to spend a week with my parents. So... happy to spend some time with the whole gang so we could bond without the pseudo shadow of classwork related stress or schedules to keep. We ended up being a gang of guys from Randy and Dom's dorm including but not limited to them plus David, myself, Antra as she'd been at lunch that day, and Becky who already knew his family as they really did know each other from when they were much younger.

It wasn't that I wanted to be the only girl; it was that I didn't feel comfortable with Antra and Becky and being pushed into a situation where we were grouped together as "the girls". Antra was cute enough but I just didn't feel any connection to her. Becky was just as much a mystery after months of intimacy with David as she had been the night of the Red House. Any time I brought her up he was dismissive so I had stopped doing it, but waiting around to start the trip they were clearly just as pally as ever. It irked me because it meant there was a relationship with feelings he was hiding or didn't want to discuss with me. Or worse yet it could be there were frequent shared activities he was hiding. I immediately chastised myself for doubting his integrity. I reminded myself I didn't share every thought with him. To want to know every detail of his days would be controlling and intrusive and I checked myself.

Still I couldn't help wondering how often did they actually hang out and could they be doing anything that motivated him to omit it for months? Or was he pre-empting my potentially emotional reaction if I might think he was leaving me out of something; or if he knew he was too close to her for my comfort? Well, come on, he couldn't possibly be doing anything wrong. He loved me right? He'd not said it in so many words but he'd demonstrated it so many times. Every one of his actions Vis a Vis me told me unequivocally he did love me. He tracked me with his eyes, he remembered what I wore, he had picked up some of my expressions, and he seemed to always know exactly where I had been. His focus on me was not that different from my obsession with him if I broke it down and analysed it bit by bit. What I felt for David was soooo strong I was sure it must be reciprocal so he surely must be beyond reproach. I pushed myself to be more grown up about it.

Couples don't have to share everything about their friends and there is nothing wrong with having friends of the opposite sex. I mean I spent loads of time with Randy and Dom and David never asked me about that in detail did he? Of course, he lived in the dorm with them and probably knew all the details anyway but that wasn't the point. The point was I was exemplifying the crazy jealous psycho bitch trains of thought the guys so often complained about. Christ sake, he'd been friends with her before he even met me. I needed to get over it. I tried not to let it be visible that I was gritting my teeth. I acted like I was very happy of the chance to get to spend time getting to know her better.

Fat chance. We split up into three cars and the guys who were driving decided one girl per car because they didn't want anyone of them stuck listening to women jabber on the whole way down. I was relieved I wouldn't have to make chit chat about makeup and gossip mag articles. Not so thrilled David was going off to the car Becky was in. I asked Randy to help me with my bag to which he shouted "I am not your packhorse Cherie! If you can't carry your own bag you should have left something behind." Randy, Dom and two guys I'd not spent too much time with up to that day – Kevin and Rich - spent the two hours singing along to the songs on the radio and arguing about when and where to stop on the way. Dom was so intent on making it as far as possible without stopping he asked me to look out the window so he could pee into a coke bottle. I wasn't sure but I supposed I was flattered he felt comfortable enough to do this with me there? I mean rather than pull over to the side of the road in last-minute desperation. Of course, Dom was bull-headed so it could simply have been dedication to the objective of going without stopping until the car was on the verge of running out of gas.

We got to the trailer park about an hour before dinner. I hadn't stopped to imagine it up to that point as I'd never been up close to a trailer let alone inside one ever before. I only realised when we were in the camp that we were all going to be rather cramped. To have a shower I'd have to get dressed and walk across a wide open public yard in the exposed outside air to a communal setup like the university dorms but without heating, doors on the cubicles or electric plugs anywhere. David clarified we weren't actually all sleeping in his mother's trailer. Most of us would have to sleep in the cars. Great. But since everybody was really only planning on one night how bad could it be? Antra made a face and Becky said who was planning on sleeping anyway with the hunt that was planned.

I wondered what Becky meant but David took me inside to meet his mother so I didn't get a chance to ask. David's mother was sitting on an orange and yellow flower-patterned sofa, surrounded by brown and gold Formica and with a brown shag carpet under her feet, hunched over a very large hook and loop rug from an arts and crafts store that she seemed hard at work on. The picture on it was of dressage riders on horses. I wondered if she'd ever been near a dressage school in her life. She said she was making a nice rug for David to have something to put next to his bed in the dorms so he didn't have to step onto the cold vinyl flooring in the middle of the night. I thought that was sweet of her but David laughed derisively like she'd said something ridiculous. His mother said well, she wanted him to have something to remind him of her when he was away from home. He could take it along wherever he went and give it to his kids when he had some. David guffawed, "My mother is making me an heirloom. HA ha ha." I didn't know his mother and couldn't know if she might just be making a show for guests like my father would have; but still my reaction was to decide David's attitude was uncharitable. I pretended to be interested in how she was doing it before saying I needed to find the washrooms to clean my hands. Walk across the alien concrete yard through a gauntlet of surly-looking unwashed overweight people sitting on plastic lawn chairs; a lot of them apparently chewing gum while also smoking cigarettes.

Dinner was an inedible buffet of refined white buns, uncooked low quality hot dogs with same day expiry date and LOTS of condiments. Apparently the trick was to drown them in sauces to disguise the taste but I couldn't stomach it. Luckily I had brought my own box of cereal, but I now had a better appreciation for why these people thought the cafeteria food was ok to eat. While I watched the others eat bottles of ketchup and mustard with bland bread they started talking about the big plan for the night. Becky had found David's cousins Frank and Jon, and they had designed a scavenger hunt for us to do in teams. I was surprised as this was a lot more initiative than I was used to from the normal group. Frank and Jon were very outgoing though. Their parents were missionaries and they'd lived most of their lives in an exotic variety of "underdeveloped" countries that I would've been afraid to be in without a security team to protect me. I supposed their outgoing nature must be the upside of moving around so much in foreign lands. For them the trailer park actually seemed to be more luxury than they were used to given the clean running water and toilets. The details of the scavenger hunt as they set them out made me realise that being a missionary's son must be akin to being a preacher's daughter. The scavenger hunt consisted of a list of items that must be collected between 8 and 11 pm; groups of four per team and any items brought back after eleven didn't count. So far ok. The issue was what was on the list. A sample:

- Hotel bible provable to be from a hotel (1 point)
- Traffic cones (1 point per)
- Bus stop sign (5 points)
- Fast food chain straw dispenser (4 points)
- Road traffic sign (public not private : 10 points)
- Cinemaplex poster from one of the films currently showing (5 points)
- Policeman's or Fireman's hat or helmet (15 points)
- Fire hose (15 points)
- Fast food chain chair (name of the specific chain omitted due to proprietary reasons : 15 points)
- Park bench (15 points)
- Payphone (20 points for the whole phone, 3 for part)
- Railroad crossing barrier (20 points)
- Slot Machine (50 points)
- Pinball Machine (50 points)
- Cash register (100 points)

- Police car lights (100 points)
- etc…

There were fifty such items on the list. All of them clearly required some deception but I thought the great majority of them required breaking some law or other if they weren't simply considered stealing. I had expected a sort of glorified Easter egg hunt but was faced with a crime spree. Dom and I looked at each other and I saw he felt the same way so we decided to be on the same team. Kevin and Rich joined us so that ruled out spending any time at all with David. David didn't waste time getting Antra and others on his team. Becky apparently went way back with Frank and Jon and the three of them were glued to each other for the remainder of the night.

When the other teams had left Dom and I looked at each other and argued about whether we should actually stay. Dom wanted to leave and go back to the dorms but he was obliged to drive Kevin and Rich so couldn't unless they agreed. I wanted to stay because I wanted to see David afterward; although I couldn't tell Dom that, I again wondered if he hadn't added 2+2. Kevin and Rich didn't seem to have the same moral issues we had. They were looking at the list saying they wished they knew the town better because we would lose time finding where the fast food places were. Since it seemed they were up for it I said to Dom we couldn't let them do it unsupervised. We both felt responsible for some reason. I said how about we each take one item then? Dom refused but he said he'd stay at the trailer park until we came back because he knew he was our ride.

Kevin, Rich and I took Dom's car and I called dibs on the hotel bible. It was easy. I went into the hotel reception and asked for one saying I was religious but had forgotten my own bible when I packed because my husband rushed me. Rich looked embarrassed and guilty so this visually backed up my story and the receptionist gave one to me without even asking if I was a guest. It had the hotel stamp inside so proven and my point was won.

Kevin found tools in the trunk of the car and said he had the next one so long as we stood around him to cover what he was doing. In a very crowded fast food joint that was apparently one of only two for a very long distance, Rich and I stood shoulder to shoulder pretending to look at the menu over the counter as Kevin knelt down behind us and unscrewed a chair from where it was bolted to the floor. I had actually started reading the menu as I'd never been in one of these places before so I didn't even realise Kevin had walked out and come back in when Rich moved me to the other side of him. Moving me was to cover Kevin unscrewing the straw dispenser from a shelf near where the chair had just been taken from.

As we walked out after that slowly and calmly I suddenly heard someone from behind the counter scream "What the fuck?" Rich and I turned around and saw a fat sweaty teenager covered in grease was looking from the space where the chair should be, then to us and then he was starting to come around the counter. I shouted "fucking MOVE Kevin". It wasn't easy though because the place was really full so we had to push a few people before getting to an open space in front of the door. As we finally ran out the door a woman in the corner distinctly said it was disgraceful to hear a young woman swearing in public. I had time to simultaneously (1) mentally condemn her for her sexism while (2) laughing at her ignorance -if only she knew what else we were doing- and (3) feeling ashamed for abetting an act of theft (4) thinking how small minded can someone be they worry about swear words at that age rather than what is actually being said or done, and (5) being scared we might get caught because the burger jockey was catching up to us fast despite his obesity and crowd of people in between all generally looking up over the counter so not getting out of his way. Maybe I was thinking other things on other levels but consciously I was aware of those. We only just made it into the car and locked the doors as he reached it and banged on the driver side windows yelling at us to stop. Kevin pulled away and we debated whether we should go straight back to the trailer park. I voted yes but Rich wanted to win and thought we needed at least one more item because we only had 20 points and a lot of the items on the list were worth that on their own. I grimaced inwardly but tried not to show it when I asked "what do you want to get then?" He wanted a road sign.

Rich actually wanted a specific road sign he'd seen on the way into town. There was a mile marker "42" just outside the trailer park and he wanted it to take home with him. So we went to get the mile marker but this was no easy feat. After 20 minutes of trying Rich decided it couldn't be unbolted or unscrewed. Then he and Kevin started to dig it up but they realised it was far too deeply embedded and it actually had concrete at the bottom of the post so might not be possible to dig up anyway. Then they decided to break it off. They started bending the post back and forth between them and after another 40 minutes of effort (it wasn't easy as it took the full strength of both of them to get it to bend each time) the post was severed and we made it back to the trailer park with just five minutes to spare. Watching the guys get the mile marker was boring as watching grass grow, but the adrenaline rush surging through me when we deposited our stuff in a pile in the middle of the compound was incredible. I'd never before felt anything like breaking the law under a deadline with a last-minute race to the finish line.

We had thirty points but we came fourth out of four groups. Clearly, we had underestimated the criminal leanings of some of our competitors. There was actually a railroad crossing barrier and a whole payphone next to Becky, Frank and Jon among a pile of lesser points items they had grabbed. Frank was bleeding out of a gash on his arm but grinning ear to ear as Jon patted him on the back. Becky had zealot admiration in her eyes as she looked at the brothers and shimmied up to kiss Frank. Another team had amassed multiple road signs apparently having gotten it down to a science (they had specialised tools because one had done work on road crews over his summers); but Frank said only one of each type item from the list counted. That's why they were second; otherwise those guys would have won. David and Antra's team was third.

Everyone seemed to have chairs, napkin holders and straw dispensers from the same two fast-food restaurants. A police car entered the trailer park just as Becky was being held aloft Frank and Jon's shoulders - bottle of cheap convenience store wine in hand - to celebrate their victory. On seeing the police car everyone scattered. Antra, Becky and a bunch of the others ran behind the communal bathrooms. I stood there like a bunny in headlights as Dom, Kevin and Rich ran the opposite direction where there was what looked like woods. I saw the sweaty overweight burger hustling employee who had run after us in the parking lot was sitting in the back seat of the police car. I figured the game was up because he would surely recognise me. I gazed over the four piles of stash and across the now people-free area between me and the police car. Practically driven by my autonomic functions I stepped forward.

David had apparently been to the left of my field of vision when he saw me starting toward the police car. He rushed up to me saying "you're going the wrong way" while he grabbed my arm and turned me around. He dragged me —still not consciously in control of what I was doing- into his mother's trailer. I was sputtering "but they've got us what's the point of trying to hide?" when he said "Shhhh, it's all misdemeanour crap and they know it. They'll just take the stuff back. We don't have to offer ourselves up." While he was saying this he bolted the door behind us. "But they've got a witness; he'll recognise me." "Not if he doesn't see you dummy. We'll just have to stay in here the rest of the night." "What about your mother?" "She's gone to BINGO and after is very likely to go to her boyfriend's place. Don't worry about her. Worry about me." He had already gotten me to step backward and sit on the ugly couch by now, and was putting my hand on his crotch. Then, with the other hand on my breast he said "What a rush huh? Frank and Jon really know how to get things going don't you think?" As I pulled him closer I said "I don't really want to think about them just now." Then he stopped talking. The way he looked at me and touched me made me feel the whole focus of his sentient mind. We'd been heavy petting for a few minutes when he pulled back again, looked me in the eyes with a very serious expression and said "I love you Cherie. You are my all." I was ecstatic. The criminal rush from before was a pathetically weak feeling compared to the thrilling rapture I felt when he said that to me. My voice was broken and hoarse when I warbled "you know I love you." He smiled sweetly and we recommenced the physical activities. Then, amazingly, we had sex that was a few notches above the sex we had been having up to then. Despite the cramped area, being vaguely uncomfortable about being in his mother's abode, the fact that I thought people must be able to hear us given the trailers were so close together; despite all of this I had the best sex of my life up to that point. Silly phrase given I'd only been sexually active for a couple of months? Maybe so, but the words, the affirmation, the declaration that he did in fact love me (not just that he thought he might but he'd decided he actually DID) was the headiest drug I'd ever known. It wasn't a mere aphrodisiac it was like a sense heightening injection that went straight to my nerve endings and my dopamine receptors. This time we were both loud. He smelled vaguely of whisky but was totally focused on us. At some point I was hazily aware of authoritative shouting and some banging on doors in the distance. Remarkably I think there was none at all on the door of the trailer we were in. I suppose there might've been and we were oblivious because there were several high magnitude orgasms for each of us that night.

David had been right about his mother. She didn't come back until the next morning after we'd already had time to get dressed and have the first coffee of the day. I was in a dreamy foggy haze and still feeling shudders of pleasure when I closed my eyes and recalled him cumming inside me. David's mother came in looking hung over and loudly complaining there wasn't enough coffee for her. This shook me out of my memorial cloud only briefly. David said to her there was a study he'd read about at college that said orgasm was the surest cure for a migraine. Hadn't her boyfriend taken care of her last night? My mouth dropped open as he grinned and winked at me. His mother shrugged it off saying it wasn't migraine she had and he'd taken plenty good care of her. I couldn't believe it. That she admitted she was hung over was remarkable to me; but this sort of exchange with a parent was beyond my comprehension. In my house a remark like David's would've been unthinkable and certainly would've been met with angry violence if it were uttered. Here it was treated like a bit of cheek. David and I most certainly came from different worlds.

When we left the trailer I was unsure what would happen vis a vis the rest of the group; but it turned out I was worried about nothing. We walked toward a café the trailer park had near the entrance and found the rest of the group still hadn't gotten up or at least hadn't shown themselves. We were awake earlier than we'd realised and I suppose that was because we hadn't really slept much anyway. When we entered the café the only other person there was a man behind the counter looking the worse for wear. The place looked like a grimy truck stop just after several tour busses have been through and before any clearing up had started: dirty glasses and greasy baskets at every table, sticky floors and empty napkin holders. It smelled like stale cigarette smoke and beer mixed with burnt fryer oil. The linoleum was a whitish grey colour and the tables were metal with hard plastic chairs around them.

The man in there, Joe, was by himself and seemed chummy with David. While he served us at the counter he complained about how the night before Frank and Jon had had a sort of rubber band fight that lasted over an hour; bothering his regular patrons as they'd been scoring each other's skill trying to bounce the bands off other people onto each other. I guessed they must know each other but David didn't introduce me so I just listened to their conversation. After much pleading with Frank and Jon it wasn't even him who'd managed to get them to stop bruising his paying customers. I guessed this meant they were special and didn't have to pay?

Becky had challenged them to a game of strip poker and that's when the three of them had sat down and played right down to their underwear right there among the punters. OK, so he also knew Becky and knew David knew her... Joe had again tried to get them to stop but they just blew him off until he'd seen Frank was telling Becky to take her bra off. Joe was speaking in an annoyed tone like what he was describing was exasperating and bothersome but not anything worse than that. That's when Joe finally physically bounced them out into the night. Wasn't it bad enough that they'd brought the police into the park making a lot of people stay away? Without them risking his license getting an underage girl to expose herself publicly like that? At that David laughed and said "Joe, didn't you realise it was Becky?" Joe's reply was sure he knew it was Becky and that's how he knew she's under age! His tone was like a person talking about children that snuck cookies they weren't allowed; like the events he was relating were NOT anything truly extraordinary just irksome.

Joe did say "for Christ's sake don't they have any sense at all?" David said probably their compass for acceptable behaviour was different because of where they'd lived. Joe replied if that was the case then they should pay more attention to the people around them. He'd seen a couple of men in there with obvious hard-ons walking around their impromptu strip poker table and he couldn't vouch for her safety. He also didn't think Frank and Jon had the brains to watch out for her. He didn't seem to feel invested in Becky's safety, just worried about whether anything might come back on him. David was sure they'd likely had their own wood to take care of and were probably only too glad Joe had pushed them out of the bar, making it possible for them to move things along (nudge nudge wink wink).

Throughout all of this interchange, I was eating pancakes and coffee Joe had served and otherwise keeping my mouth shut. I tried to look down at my plate and the table but was forced to look at Joe and David periodically to check if I was interpreting their expressions correctly. David didn't find any of what he'd heard abnormal but did seem quite amused. I was still in shock at the chasm between what they seemed nonplussed or just mildly hacked off about, versus what in my neighbourhood growing up would have warranted serious reprimand and counselling about appropriate behaviour (if not being reported to protective services). I was about to say as much when from behind us Frank said yes indeed he was grateful to Joe for pushing them out the door and into the welcoming warm sheets of his dear uncle's trailer. Joe said he had better have put them in the wash and I realised Joe must be their guardian while they were here, and must be some relation of David's since Frank and Jon were his cousins. I couldn't believe it. Their own relative had actually let them play strip poker in public and had only chided them to get out of there when the girl they were with was finally getting naked, and he assumed they'd had sex and didn't have any reservations or judgements to make about it. Implausible but in this case true. Frank looked at me and asked what I thought of his uncle's pancakes. I smiled and gave a thumbs up because my mind was still whirring with the idea that his uncle did not have any qualms about Frank sleeping with Becky in his uncle's bed.

Then Jon and Becky came in with their arms around each other; which was confusing to me. Hadn't she spent the night with Frank? I was musing this and looking at Frank when Jon said to David I looked like I was up for it. "Up for what?" I asked smiling. "Oh honey" Frank said "you're not my type." David told them to shut up and leave me alone. I didn't understand what they were talking about.

Joe asked Becky how she'd slept as he gave her a coffee. Jon said she hadn't slept she'd been moaning all night. I said "oh Becky, are you ok? Do you want an ibuprofen or something?" At this, she, Frank and Jon all looked at me like I was insane and Becky nearly shouted with an unmistakeably incredulous tone "Jesus Cherie, you really are an idiot." David just smiled and said "actually, she's a good girl". "Too right" said Joe; "she has as much business being here with you lot as a bottle of Bollinger Rose would behind my bar". Joe was pointing behind him at a small shelf of cheap whisky and vodka bottles. Becky's face had changed to a kabuki illustration of ANGRY. She gritted "Fuck you Joe," finished her coffee in one gulp and walked out.

Jon said "Christ Joe, way to go. I haven't seen her that pissed off since she came to see us in Morocco." Joe still sounded like he was philosophizing more than concerned when he replied "she needs to take stock of what she's doing. I'm not her guardian but she's on a poor path. I'd say the same for you two if it weren't for the fact you're boys and you can get away with it. But she's closing down her options fast." David's face was a cross between musing and confusion for a very brief moment before saying "Whatever Joe. You're an old man. It's not the same for people our age. She's old enough to make her own decisions. Anyway, what happened in Morocco? I've never heard that story?"

Frank explained when she'd gone to visit them in Morocco she'd been dressed pretty inappropriately given how ultraconservative that society is. Nothing like what she's wearing here today just, you know, showing too much leg and cleavage. At the bazaar a guy tried to trade a camel for her. Frank had said "What do I want with a camel? Offer me something interesting." At that Becky had hit Frank so hard on the back of his head his vision had gone blurry for a moment. On seeing that the Moroccan man changed his offer to a pair of goats, at which Becky had screamed out loud. While she was screaming bloody murder because Frank wasn't telling this guy to go to hell, the guy took the offer off the table. Becky's screaming had attracted the local police, who made Frank 'gag his whore' before they took care of her. She'd spent the following two days pretending Frank didn't exist and speaking only to Jon. She didn't feel any of it was her own fault. She didn't forgive Frank for gagging her and didn't understand she'd escaped a much worse fate. She had thought Frank should've argued with the police to make it clear she was no whore. Frank trying to explain things were different in Morocco hadn't made her any less angry. Becky seemed to think the whole world should adhere to her perceptions of what is appropriate for a woman to do. There Jon interrupted to say not that they had any issue with women being equal and definitely none with sexual liberation, but you have to know where you are and in Morocco you do NOT argue with the police.

All of this was fascinating to me. Not least of which was the idea of spending time abroad unsupervised. It wasn't really real to me though because it was so far outside my own world I couldn't grasp it at all. It was as the years passed that looking back on it I realised Becky and her beaus were either extremely progressive or they were very lost. It probably was true that her sexual liberation could only be appreciated or considered a possibility within the American context. Such behaviour anywhere else in the wide world at that age in that decade would have - if it were known - meant her being automatically written off from many areas of society. I didn't comment though. Who was I to comment on what someone else did with their own body? It was, in my mind, her own choice. She apparently did things I thought were repulsive but the world is made up of people of many different tastes and it wasn't for me to impose mine on anyone. Then I started thinking again about Becky and David and thought if he'd spent a lot of time with her he'd probably had sex with her too, but maybe it didn't mean that much given she seemed to have sex quite freely. Maybe it did, I couldn't really tell because her behaviour was so beyond me. I realised David was watching my face, analysing my silent musings. He looked sad when he said "Come on Cherie; let's go find Dom so you can get back to the dorms."

The rest of the spring break was pretty uneventful given I was on my own for most of it. It was peaceful to have everything to myself, and jarring when everybody else came back to campus. We quickly got back into our weekly routines.

The first night David and I were alone again he told me his mother had realised he was in love when they'd decorated their Easter eggs. They decorated Easter eggs in the trailer park? It sounded like LITTLE HOUSE ON THE PRARIE to me. I had never done anything like that in my house. We'd never even done anything like that in school because I went to non-denominational schools where religious-type activities were shunned. He said yes, they decorated Easter eggs in the trailer park and hid them for the younger kids to find. I smiled and said "tell me more." He'd done six eggs with the Batman symbol in different colours when his mother said to do something different because the girls might not like Batman. Then he'd written Cherie inside a purple heart and his mother remarked it MUST be love given I was right up there with his favourite superhero. I laughed but it actually made me feel warm inside to know he'd not only thought of me but he'd exposed his feelings to his mother. I was so sure of his love for me now I felt he was a part of me.

I didn't look to the future with him because it wasn't in my nature to plan an imaginary wedding like the other girls on the dorm floor did. I certainly never daydreamt about myself walking down the aisle. Some of them confessed they did often; however, and had even identified what specific invitation pattern or what particular menu items they would have on their 'special day'. After a lifetime with my parents I didn't believe in marriage. I did, however, believe that two people who love each other stay together. I'd seen that in plenty of movies. Growing up, my confidence in the rudimentary authenticity behind fiction nurtured my belief happy love must exist somewhere. I mean art is supposed to reflect life, right?

Now I was sure I had it. LOVE! Blissful love. I was so lucky. People can spend their entire lives not knowing what love is; never meeting anyone who they feel for sincerely, but I was living love every day. Not a crush, not lust, but honest affection with tenderness, friendship and passion. What it is in fact supposed to be between two people. If you don't have the whole hog you are settling for less. Some people may do that but I wouldn't have to because I most definitely had the whole hog. David and I thought in sync and often said the same things at the same time. We understood each other's facial expressions in a way no one around us came close to. We had the same ideas and for the most part the same tastes. No one else had ever watched out for me the way he did when he tried to explain things to me or give me advice. Advice on how to take what people said, explaining what might motivate them to say it. Always trying to make sure I fit in and making me know I was in his thoughts.

Sometimes I thought he might be reading my mind. For instance, once I couldn't open my dorm room door and couldn't figure out why. I was just standing there trying the key looking perplexed and thinking 'why doesn't the key work?' and David said out loud "because you used it to wipe paint off your shoe this morning." I was astonished. He was right. Earlier that day I had stepped on a freshly painted crosswalk and I'd used the edge of the key to scrape the reflective paint off the heel of my shoe and there it was in the groove of the key. It had solidified rock hard and I had to ask around for a screwdriver to force the paint out of the groove in the key. Clearly he must've watched me scraping my shoe while I was unawares, and he too would've been thinking 'why can't she open the door?' but it was spooky. Either way, it showed (a) he liked watching me come and go enough to spy on me, and (b) the way we thought was on the same lines. You may think no, probably just a coincidence he happened to observe you doing that on that particular day, but this sort of thing was far too frequent for it to be simply coincidental he'd seen me. Someone else might've stood there saying "what is wrong with you?" or "forget how to turn a key?" or "did they change the locks on you?" but he literally answered the question I had thought to myself.

The next two and a half months – the time between spring break and the summer holiday - flew by for me. I breezed through classes and was pretty continually on a happy and contented high. It became second nature to carry on with two separate lives. In one I had a public face with my friends and the outside world, where I went to class and tried to care about my future. In the world I in fact cherished, it was just David and me in a time bubble, and I wouldn't have cared at all if the outside world disappeared from any existence that crossed paths with my own.

I thought David would make an excellent spy because I never saw even an inkling of what we did on his face when we were in front of other people. I wondered whether other people didn't think this about him when he organised a GOTCHA type game across the campus where people were assigned targets to hit using paintball pistols. He was ruthless. No one ever saw him coming because he'd shoot them midsentence while he had their attention distracted away from himself. Of course, he was an acting major. I didn't have that kind of talent to hide what I was thinking and feeling but I did my best and when something slipped it was usually explained away as being something else or just my now legendary general overly sensitive nature.

Still, never having any public acknowledgement did bother me sometimes. One night in the Irish bar, we were standing on opposite sides of the group of people we'd gone therewith. I had my back to the room and was facing the group, talking to Randy, when a smelly drunk guy started rubbing up against my back. I tried to move away, thinking it must just be really crowded but when I did move, I saw it wasn't actually crowded enough for that. It was only ten pm and the place was not that full so early. I threw the guy a look. I was ticked off but turned back to Randy to continue blathering about whatever it was we were talking about. Then the drunk jerk put his head on my shoulder and said "Come on baby, you want to go home with me. I've got a dick like a man-hole cover. Not that long but sooooo wide it'll blow your mind." My eyes registered shock and disgust and I saw David on the other side of the group watching and laughing at my reaction. He can't have known what the drunk bastard said but he did see how the guy was hanging on me. I stooped and shifted to one side to get the guy off me. He smelled foul. I was gagging from repulsion when I felt wet and realised he'd either drooled or spewed on my shoulder. It was wet but I couldn't tell with what. I screamed "oh my god! Randy, what did this asshole do to my shoulder?" David laughed out loud at that. The guy next to him thought he'd been funny but I could see David was looking straight at me. Randy inspected my shoulder and confirmed it was mostly just drool; just as the drunk idiot tried to re-position himself to wrap his arms around me.

Note: no one else told this guy to walk away or leave me be because back then if a girl was in a bar this was part of the risk she took. A caveat might exist if she was visibly in the company of a specific male as that could work as a deterrent. However; it was perpetually open season on any apparently unattached girl. Unwanted attention from men was normal; especially if the men were drunk. Any female who tried to fob them off or tell them to leave her alone was just inviting more aggressive focus from the guy if not insult. In my head, I wished David might see how uncomfortable this jerk made me and do something. Anything at all would've worked for me, from a sympathetic facial expression to an arm pushing the offensive drunk away from me. Nothing was forthcoming aside from him secretly laughing at my situation from the other side of the group. Times like that I would feel low and sad but still not anywhere in the vicinity of how unhappy my home life had been before going to university. By comparison, even a shitty moment like being harassed by the warped pervert in the bar was a happy occasion.

I said "That's it; I'm leaving before I ralph all over this creep. Randy will you walk with me?" Randy went about halfway with me; just to make sure the drunk from the bar wasn't following, and then went back to the bar. I put my clothes in the laundry and showered to wash the icky feeling away. About an hour and a half after I'd gotten back David knocked on the door. When I opened it he said he was glad to find me alone because he thought he'd lost me for the night to the advances of the man in the bar. I was angry he could make light of it. I told him to go home because I was into the book I had been reading and was enjoying the quiet. He just laughed again when he saw I was incensed. He put his hand inside my robe as he said "oh Cherie, you should've stayed a bit longer." I tried stepping back away from his arm but he took it as an invitation to step into the room. He was still smiling as he said "They threw the douche bag out after he let rip a massive fart that everyone heard in a break between songs." He tried to close his arms around me as I tried to keep him at arm's length. "They threw him out for farting?" "No! Haha! Everyone looked at him when they heard the sound and we saw crap was seeping onto his shoes from his pant legs and his whole backside was … just really nauseating." He pulled me toward him with force now; his hands on either side of my waist, and I wasn't strong enough to fend this off. David continued "Seriously. He was only there about 10 more minutes. When I came here he was passed out on the sidewalk." I shivered in revulsion at the thought of the spectacle he described. It pissed me off that that asshole was free to drool on me, and men would only find his actions offensive enough to spark action when they involved spreading faeces and odour. I wanted to take another shower. As I thought about it I started to get livid, but David made shooing noises and enveloped me. He started kissing me and this distracted me. The longer we kissed the less I thought of anything other than David. The rest of the world just slid into nothingness as the sensation of David washed through me. His smell was delicious. I forgot about the drunken sod. The bastard could drown in his own puke for all I cared (he didn't though – something like that would've been in the paper next day for sure).

Toward the end of the last month of the semester I was dreading the arrival of the summer holiday. I didn't fancy the idea of returning to the relative imprisonment of months with my parents after living like an autonomous adult all semester. Randy, Dom and David all started commenting on how I'd lost my appetite at different meals and I'd have to remind them that the food was awful. The truth was they would catch me distracted instead of eating. I'd lose the thread of conversations and Randy took to calling me Gilligan because I'd misunderstand what he was on about. I couldn't stand the idea of having to go back to having my every single word and movement controlled and was trying to think of ways to stay longer on campus or return earlier in the fall. David had a bit of an idea about what I was not looking forward to but didn't really know or understand. Despite talking about everything and anything we cared to; I never wanted to discuss the hell that was my parental domicile. That would have made me a victim in his eyes or pitiful or damaged or certainly less desirable. I do think he knew; though, that if I hadn't told my parents about him it was because I never told my parents anything about anything that mattered to me. That would've been an invitation to derision, disparagement, and efforts to stop me doing or having whatever it was I'd expressed enjoyment of or interest in.

In the last week of the semester I'd finished all my exams but had lied about this to my parents so I might stay longer at the dorms. I essentially gave myself a full week of holiday before going home by pretending my last exam was on the last possible day rather than when it actually was. All my friends hated me for this because I spent the days distracting them from their last-minute cramming and harangued them to go out with me until they finally gave in. David, of course, didn't have to cram for anything. I mean, what sort of study can you do for interpretive exercises once you've memorised your recitation? He could think about how he wanted to express himself from anywhere. A bar or laying on the grass in the quad were just as good for that as holed up in a dorm or study room. Actually, they were likely better as he could observe the people walking by and think about how to incorporate them into his intern. We had a really fantastic and fun week; although the other people around us dwindled as they started going home.

On the last night all of my friends had gone; both the guys and the ones from my own dorm. It was just me and David left. We went to a local restaurant for dinner and it was like an actual date. I'd never been on a proper date before with anyone. He dressed up and came to get me at six pm with a rose in his hand. I had made a massive effort with my makeup and hair, and was wearing a figure-hugging flowy black dress. He said I looked beautiful. We walked arm in arm across the quad and into town. He made a point of opening doors for me and bowing as I went through them; which was a bit annoying at first but in the end made me giggle. Unfortunately, I seemed to have some sort of bug. The food was highly recommended and rated and David had no problem scarfing his down but the smell was making my stomach turn. I didn't manage to eat much of the main course but I wasn't really thinking about it because David had taken my hand and was holding it on top of the table. When desert came I had no problem with the ice cream and realised he was just watching me eat. I looked up from my empty desert place and he was staring intently in my eyes.

He apologised I hadn't liked the food. He had wanted the night to be the perfect send off since we couldn't see each other over the summer. I said not to be silly it had been perfect I just seemed to have some nausea. I had probably been fighting off some bug for weeks come to think of it; the smell of the cafeteria had been making my stomach churn as well. After dinner we went to a cosy club that neither of us had ever been to with anyone else, and had a drink and listened to the music but didn't manage to talk much. Thinking about being away from him made me want to cry and I couldn't think of what else to talk about. When I asked him what he'd do all summer he said his plans were same as every year; nothing special to discuss there. We realised we didn't want to be out and about so we went back to my room and after some tenderness we fell asleep in each other's arms. Next morning he woke me up for more before leaving. It was difficult to let him go and he didn't seem to want to leave either, but finally he had to or he'd have missed his ride.

About thirty minutes after I'd closed the door on David my mother was screaming in my ear asking how was it possible I wasn't ready. She didn't want to have to spend the whole day waiting for me to get dressed. She was also suspicious that no one else was around on the floor and started asking why was my last test so much later than everyone else's? One more hour later her car was full of my stuff and we started driving back home. She hadn't let me have time to shower so I was wearing dirty jeans and a t-shirt and could still smell David on me as I looked out the window. Watching the fields go by I started counting down the days until the summer break would be over.

When I was four; one day out shopping in the mall my parents started having a row right in the middle of a shoe store. Mother wanted a pair of shoes she'd seen and Father didn't want to pay for them; saying she had too many shoes and she never wore most of them. I took the opportunity to hide behind the next display aisle. I just wanted to get away from them and hoped they'd not notice I was gone. I breathed in the smell of faux leather and rubber and shortly I knew I was right. When Father finally won the argument, threatening to smack Mother right there in front of everyone in the store if she didn't shut the fuck up, they left the shop and left me behind. I saw them go, waited another while (don't know how long but it seemed like a long time – I was only four and didn't have a watch), then went out of the shop and started walking through the mall. I headed toward a candy store and on the way found a dollar bill someone had dropped. It was my lucky day and I was free. I was trying to buy gummy sweets when my mother whacked me on the arm asking where had I been? I was not to leave her side. She dragged me by the forearm back to the car where my father was waiting. Then he hit me so hard across the face one of my lose baby teeth fell out. In the car on the way home I realised I'd lost the dollar as the server at the candy counter had kept it.

One day in late spring when I was five; we went to an authentic Black Hawk Native American Indian powwow. I was entranced by multi-coloured beadwork and fantastic feathers. The chanting, dancing and drumming was enthralling. I fancied living in the wilderness wearing slippers and suede all day every day and dancing around a campfire. I snuck into the edge of the woods, hoping my parents would leave and then the Indians might adopt me. I waited for the noise of cars and crowds leaving to die down. Then I peeked out from behind a tree on the edge of the clearance. A striking young woman with all pink and white beading spied me and asked me if I was lost. I said no, I'm running away because I want to join your tribe. She looked concerned, confused and amused all at once. She said I couldn't stay with them because I wasn't one of them. I had parents and must return to them. I was adamant I didn't want to go back to my parents, and started crying when she insisted the Indians didn't want me as I'd surely be more trouble than I was worth. My crying immobilised me and she took advantage of that to pick me up and carry me to the car park. My father was screaming at my mother for not keeping better control of me.

When the pink lady was able to distract their attention long enough to hand me over my father yanked me by the wrist and spanked me right there in the parking lot; yelling about how I'd embarrassed them by running off. One of the men from the tribe told him to take it easy, so my father told that man to fucking mind his own business. When we got home he whaled on me so hard I wasn't allowed to go to kindergarten the whole next week lest someone say something about my bruises. When he was done beating me he forced me to kiss him and say "I love you daddy" and "thank you for teaching me a lesson". This was his favourite way to conclude a walloping. I was always made to show affection and gratitude for having been thrashed. If I ever refused he'd lose his temper and the belting and hiding would start all over again, and last until I was willing to submit. When the bruising had reduced I went back to kindergarten wearing long sleeves and ankle-length pants despite it being a sweltering hot spring; and was told to say I'd had bronchitis.

On the morning of my sixth birthday I was excited because in school we had done an exercise in spelling where we'd had to spell things like present, card, cake, wrapping, bow, happy, candle, birthday, party, balloon, etc. Part of the exercise was to draw pictures to show the meaning of each word and I had let my imagination get the better of me. I bounced out of bed and was practically jumping in place as I had breakfast; but nothing happened. It was the same breakfast as every other day. No one said "happy birthday". There was no wrapping paper to be seen, no bows, nothing. I was only just that very day six but knew better than to provoke anything so I kept my mouth shut. But it was too difficult for me at that age. In the car on the way to school I started crying from disappointment. My mother actually didn't even notice until she was unlocking the door for me to get out. She was leaning across me to get the knob when she asked what was wrong with me. I wailed "you didn't remember my birthday!" She looked startled for a brief millisecond then said "Get over yourself. Who cares about your birthday? Go to school." She opened the door and started pushing me in the back until I got out and stood up. Then she kept yelling for me to go until I was far enough away from the door that she could close it. She drove off and my birthday wasn't mentioned again at all that year by anyone.

After that school year ended the parents started shipping me around between my uncles, aunts, their cousins, etc. but I was still made to go back to the parents every summer and Christmas. I hated the holidays other people anticipate and enjoy, because for me they meant returning to a jail with a psychopath warden.

The summer break meant three months of listening to yelling matches between my parents when not trying to avoid being smacked around or debased. Even though I had a driver's license I was not trusted to use the car unaccompanied and my father would not let me meet up with friends from high school; including Randy and Dom, because I needed to help my mother around the house. She wasn't all there to be honest, but certainly was enough to rat me out if I did anything that might make her day more stressful than 16 hours in bed with intermittent tea brakes. I think her urges to get me in trouble were driven by the desire to get focus shifted off her; to make my father scream at and hit someone else so she could have a break. So I made my face stony and planned to just wait it out until I could go back to university. It was easier to get through the days than in previous years though as I'd think about the nights before the break began – replaying it – and looked forward to seeing David when we got back to campus. My mother remarked I didn't have much of an appetite, and the fact was my stomach was constantly unsettled. I felt jumpy like my skin was crawling. I also had a lot of gas that I thought must be down to nerves. I guessed it was just that much more difficult to be back there given I'd found happiness in the dorms.

Weeks into the break I started to feel a lot of pain between my legs that I couldn't understand and had a lot of discharge. I say between my legs. I mean in my genitalia but I still wasn't woman enough to refer to it like that at this point. Honestly, I now know if you aren't adult enough to call parts by their proper names you probably aren't adult enough to be mashing them up against the opposite sex. But at this point I was still a teenager and ignorant enough I thought maybe it was a really bad yeast infection. However, it didn't go away when I treated it and then the pain kept getting worse. I was wary of saying anything at home, ruing the fact that whatever it was couldn't have appeared when I was on campus and might've been dealt with by the aloof campus clinic staff. If I saw someone while home it would have to be a doctor I'd known all my life and who often went to dinner with my parents.

Just being at home was a nightmare with my father getting aggressive because I wasn't grateful enough for whatever he'd done to facilitate my life. My mother was in hysterics because cooking for an extra person (myself) was too stressful for her and she felt she ought to have a maid to do this sort of thing or at least we should have a caterer. That set my father into a rage. On the fourth of July I was in no state to be around anyone and absolutely suffered throughout the excruciatingly forced block party barbeque organised in my neighbourhood; where I had to make small talk with the "adults" because people my age had all gone off to a party that I wasn't given permission to go to. As soon as I'd finished what I figured was maximum duty of sixty minutes I slinked back to our house to the basement to avoid everyone by saying I had a project to work on. Within 30 minutes I wretched up the entire dinner. My mother found out when she came after me to make me go back outside for the fireworks. She saw I was sick and took that personally. I was too nauseous and tired to say anything so just went to bed.

The next morning the pain in my pelvis was really strong so I got a mirror to look, saw sores all over my nether regions and freaked out. I snuck to the basement while my parents were still asleep to call Doctor Glenda Cooper, OBGYN. Dialling the phone I had a pit in my stomach like I was perpetrating an offence and my voice was croaky. I whispered pleading for her to see me and please please please could she not tell my parents. Glenda made me breathe deep, stop whining and say clearly why I'd woken her up on her day off. When I did this she sighed and said she'd come pick me up in 45 minutes. My heart broke to hear the disappointment in her voice as she said we'd tell my parents she was taking me to a show in the art gallery. This was plausible as there was one on over the break and neither of my parents had the slightest interest in that kind of thing. My heart pounded as I thought if she was disappointed but still helping me in this way then something must really be wrong.

Glenda Cooper had always taken an interest in what she considered bright undervalued girls. I think it was a personal ambition of hers to boost more women into professions as she gave talks in schools and funded a scholarship. She told me once I wasn't a recipient of one because I was too lazy to apply. She also did a lot of charity work abroad rather than take holidays; which may be partly why she was put out I was asking her go into the office on her day off. Anyway, she was an oasis from the storm on many an awful night out with my parents to society dinners but I will never be able to repay what she did for me.

She took me to her office; that was actually closed for the week, and had me strip and lay down.

She gasped when she saw the sores and asked what the hell had I been doing? How was it possible that I'd only been away a few months and I'd managed to get not one but two STDs and this was certainly the first and most definitely the last time she'd hide something like this from my parents or anyone's parents for that matter. My being 17 didn't mean she had no responsibility to them if I was putting myself in danger. Then she breathed deep and said "Cherie, whoever it is that gave this to you, to give you TWO STDs they might've given you anything. You might've gotten HIV. I'm going to have to test you for everything. I've never seen so many sores like this. It's not even a common disease over here. Whoever gave you this has either been travelling around the east or sleeping with prostitutes." Then she decided she would need to take a photo to send to the clinic at my university - not to worry no one would ever know it was me – as chancroid was indeed rare and they might not know how to diagnose it properly. I didn't just have that though, I also had gonorrhoea for Christ's sake. Unbelievable. Had I been sleeping around? Maybe I wasn't the kind of girl she thought I was after all. I was lucky though that she'd worked in clinics in Asia because an inexperienced eye might have misdiagnosed and time was of the essence.

The whole time she was going on I was falling apart inside but she couldn't see my face because she was staring at, swabbing then photographing my parts. My chest cavity was a black hole that pulled stronger and stronger with each word Glenda said. I felt caustically empty as I listened and each breath was a massive chore. My pain turned to bewilderment then despair. The incubation period for these bacteria, for me to have the symptoms, was a couple of weeks; so David must have been with prostitutes (or any other whore I thought but Glenda insisted it was very rare – like I'd won some sort of lottery) weeks before my romantic summer break send-off. So after basically living with me for five and a half months in the same bed and having told me he loved me; but before the sweet end of semester send off and the last times we'd slept together, he'd been with someone else of nefarious past. So he'd waylaid somewhere that was disease central; and come back to me to pass it on while telling me how much he loved me. My shame was boundless. The sorrow made me break out in tears. I tried to sob as quietly as I could. The fact that she said it was common in the east to me said it probably came via Frank or Jon, via Becky to David. I fought the train of thought, but it was logical and it was at least easier to accept David cheating on me with Becky than possible alternatives. I loved him. How could he do this to someone who loved him so much unless he didn't love them back? He can't possibly really love me to have done this. The logic pulverised my lungs as acid dissolved my body cavity. David said he loved me but he had sex with others too. It wasn't possible. They were mutually exclusive concepts in my mind.

Glenda realised I was crying when she finished the photos; or maybe she realised before that but let me cry a bit, and then took blood samples before telling me to get dressed. She certainly wasn't going to let me off the hook just because I felt sorry for myself. I'd been irresponsible, put myself in danger, clearly lacked judgement and must never ever ever again have sex without a condom but preferably not without seeing a negative HIV test. At least not until I was much older and committed to somebody I was in love with. This made me wail. I'd only been with the one guy and I was in love with him. I'd trusted him. He was a part of me and I couldn't understand how it could be true but the evidence was clear –apparently- that he should not have been trusted.

Glenda now looked sad but just sighed and said we should go to the pharmacy together and she'd drop the swabs and blood at the hospital lab while we were there to make sure all the results were back as soon as possible. Then she got out a textbook full of photographs and walked me through them. I should know what these conditions look like, and certainly be able to recognise them in myself or at least know not to wait so long before seeking help. This was the first time I'd ever seen penises aside from David's and they looked repulsive and angry, weeping fluids, covered in sores and bumps, swollen and misshapen. For a short while my mind was distracted but when she closed the book it started whirring again doing the timeline that led to me having these conditions. A chorus of "he doesn't love me" kept repeating in a loop underneath my recursive analysis of the timeline.

At the hospital I heard her conversation with the pharmacist while I was waiting outside the door. She was exasperated. How was it possible a girl with an exclusive private education could be so ignorant about something so important? The pharmacist said it was more a reflection on the educational system than my fault. Glenda gave me two courses of antibiotics and then we did go to the art show to make sure the cover story was complete. She said she'd let me know if I needed to do anything else but if I followed the antibiotic regimen I should be fine in a few weeks. And make sure I told the person who'd given it to me as soon as possible to stop the chain.

I hid the pills, the emotional destruction and the physical pain from my parents. It hurt to walk up and down the stairs, to pee, to be in front of other people and to pretend like I wanted to do anything other than curl up in a ball in my bed or just die. It hurt to breathe and it hurt to think. Over and over in my mind I was replaying the night before the break began; mentally analysing David's face and every touch, and then remembering the incubation timeline and the book of awful photos Dr Cooper showed me. Those diseased pictures were now ingrained in my mind and they crept into the memories of sex with David. I had thought he loved me. I loved him. How can a person be so in love and it be all one sided? It didn't sink in and my mind just kept going round in circles.

The next evening my parents went out to dinner I stayed behind saying I felt fluey; which they had no problem believing since I had no appetite. When I'd seen their car go down the street I called the number I'd written down the night we'd gone to David's mom's trailer. I thought I probably wasn't supposed to have kept the number so he might see this as an infraction. As I dialled the phone I felt like I was committing a felony; heart in my stomach and feeling hollow, my ears pounding when David's mother answered. I was hoarse at first but after a couple of tries managed to ask to speak with him. The mother flat out refused to get him to the phone. I told her three times it was really important and I needed to speak with him but she wouldn't get him unless I told her what the problem was. Finally I did tell her he'd given me a disease and he needed to get checked by a doctor. She refused to believe this, and said why did I think I'd gotten it from him? Pissed off now she was being such a fucking royal bitch I screamed "Because I've not been with anyone else" and hung up. To top it off that evening I started having the period to end all periods. A clot like a small omelette pan came out of me and I felt suddenly a teeny bit physically better but I had to get a good look at it. I looked at it in the white porcelain bowl wondering how the hell was it possible to have such a large clot? It was just one more bewildering item on the list of things happening to or coming out of my body.

Two days later I got a phone call from Dr Cooper's secretary to tell me I was pregnant. I said that cannot be because I am having my period right now. But the receptionist repeated my test had just come in this morning and she re-read my name and date of birth then said positive. I whimpered please can I speak to Glenda? Dr Cooper? Please? When I was put through Glenda apologised saying the nurse should not have called me because she was going to do this herself. The test indicated I was about eight weeks pregnant so if I was bleeding I needed to go back in. At this point I was numb. My god, I'd gotten pregnant. I'd not felt any different, or maybe I was confusing the hormones with my feelings for David. Was that why I'd been nauseous? The black hole just kept sucking more of me with it and I sank into a chair because I couldn't bear the effort of standing. It was a miracle my father was out back when the receptionist had called. He had a habit of listening in anytime anyone called and I don't know what I'd have done or what he might've done if he'd heard that news.

In order to get my mother to drive me to Glenda's office I made pretence that I'd kept Glenda's glasses in my purse and that was why they'd called. Thank god she didn't ask to see them. I asked my mother to wait in the car because it would surely be only a minute. The heavily pregnant women in the waiting room eyed me evilly as the receptionist made a fuss while skipping me to the front of the line. The receptionist was flustered and sorry for being the one to give me such news; she hadn't realised what she was doing when she read the result. Glenda said she was very sorry for me and needed to make sure I was ok physically and everything was clearing up properly before I went back to university. She had me strip to do a quick exam but this time she only said the necessary to do the exam until she asked me to dress and sit down in a chair by her desk. She offered me a box of tissues and a glass of water. When I was sitting quietly she said there was no mistake in the test. I had been pregnant but seemed to have miscarried. Had I had unusual or very large clots? Uh huh. "Oh Cherie, well, this can sometimes go unnoticed when it happens early on." It was likely the miscarriage was due to the gonorrhoea. She gave me a box of sedatives she said was safe to take so long as I didn't have more than one a day. It would last me until I got back to campus but if I wasn't ok I could always call her and she'd be happy to help me however she could.

Glenda hugged me and said I'd get past this and to take care of myself. She was so sorry for me it just made me feel more shame and worthlessness. She said I had a really bright future ahead of me if I learned from this and stayed out of trouble. I would need to have periodic tests for HIV though, as it could be latent for a long time before showing up. She let me stay in her office until the puffiness and redness on my face died down and then I went back out to my mother and told her I'd been held up because Glenda had been in the middle of an exam and the nurse made me wait to see her because she wanted to say goodbye in person. To this day I believe Dr Cooper kept my secret.

I passed the days left until returning to campus completely numb. Being the time of year it was there wasn't much avoiding my parents except by going into the basement to sew but I ran out of cloth. Thankfully we watched a lot of television in my house so it helped my parents weren't actually looking at me that much. I blocked out my own thoughts while we watched banal comedies most of which I'd seen repeated at regular intervals over years. I tried to concentrate on memorising and repeating the lines. Every time I closed my eyes I'd see the clot floating in the white porcelain bowl; or the pictures of diseased genitals. At night I couldn't sleep. In the morning it was all I could manage to get out of bed before one of my parents dragged me out of it by my hair.

I'd used up the sedatives by the time I was on the bus to go back to campus so my first objective – after filling a prescription for contraceptive pills when the campus health service denied me any more sedatives – was to find Randy and Dom and get blind drunk. Randy had made cash working on a building crew and was tan as a raisin. Dom had been working in an ice cream parlour and had gained ten pounds. They wanted to wait around for other people and make a big 'gang's back together' sort of an outing; but I pushed hard that not everyone was back and we'd see everyone on the weekend anyway. We didn't go to the Irish bar because we thought for sophomore year we should try something new; and this was good as no one thought to look for us anywhere other than the Irish bar. Randy and Dom caught me up on their summers of hanging out at pools and playing sports when they weren't working.

I said nothing at all about my own summer. Randy and Dom didn't find that odd as I'd never spoken much about my home life with them. They'd met my father once or twice so knew better than to ask about anything if I wasn't telling. After we were caught up we started playing quarters and talking about science fiction programmes we'd watched. In that we had similar tastes. Then the night turned into a blur as I had lost my resistance to alcohol over the summer at home and; let's face it the aim was to get blind drunk anyway.

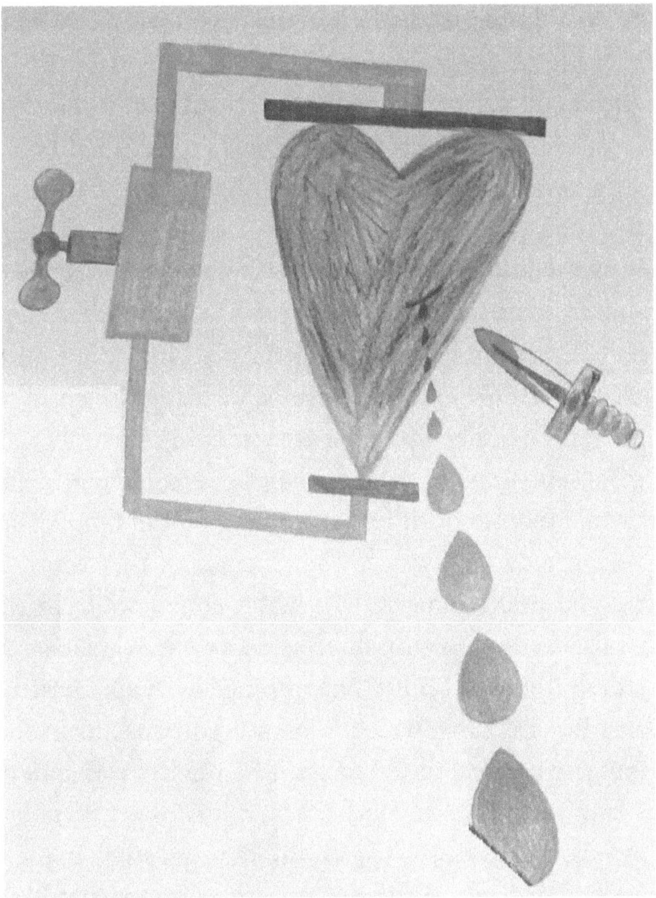

My second significant crash was at age 33 shortly after I learned a friend had died of colon cancer; although I don't think that was a factor, it is how I remember what time of year it was. It was midway through June and I had been unemployed for months after completing an MBA, had been offered minimum wage jobs but no better and had one week of money left. Finally, I found a job that would pay me the same as what I had made before starting the MBA; working in a pork processing plant doing mundane paperwork 13 hours a day in an industrial park with no access by public transport. It was at least 20 minutes' drive from any decent restaurant or shop but about 40 from my flat.

On the way home from the interview, knowing I would have to do this like it or not, I went into a sort of autopilot as I made a grocery list in my head and decided to get it while I still had a chance. Turning into a roundabout, I had been on countless times I sped up a bit then skidded on dust and gravel on the side of the road. I tried to correct but couldn't then tried to brake but too late. The car rolled onto the crash railing in the meridian then almost rolled over a second time but teetered and settled back to the centre. I had my seatbelt on so while the car needed extensive body work I got away with a bone bruise in my chest, a knocked elbow and two months of being driven to and from work by my retired father while the car was being fixed.

The most embarrassing part of that day was having to stand next to the car while thousands of Friday evening outing families snailed by gawking on their delayed way to the cinemaplex that was next to the grocery store I'd been going to. The whole time I waited I was trying to swat bugs away and off my fluorescent yellow regulation road side accident jacket; thinking I must look unhinged waving my arms around like that standing next to a wreck. I knew a guy working at the cinema a block from my car and texted to see if he might be able to give me a ride home but no. It took my father two hours to get there because he watched the end of the football game and then got stuck in the traffic I'd caused. I in fact had to pay the city to replace the crash railing despite the spot apparently being a common site for loss of control and the barrier still not being replaced well over a year after I paid for it.

When I woke up with a hangover I wanted to throw up but was too tired and despite the spinning room and my queasy stomach managed to pass out again. When I woke up the second time it was Sharon knocking at the door for me to go to lunch but I managed; despite what felt like a massive clump of bloody cotton wool in my mouth and not being able to lift my head, to say I wasn't hungry and could she just bring me a bagel. When Sharon and Gail came back at one thirty in the afternoon to give me smuggled (there was a penalty for taking food out of the cafeteria) bagels, peanut butter and cream cheese my hangover had worn off but I felt no better. Sharon was disappointed I hadn't taken her along on the night out with Randy and Dom. Gail didn't care because she'd sent the night with Jeff making up for the time lost over the break; despite them having visited each other every other week during the summer months. That meant Sharon had spent most of the night by herself in the downstairs lounge watching TV. I apologised to Sharon and said we'd been in such a hurry we were toasted by the time we realised it was just myself, Dom and Randy.

The three of us sat on the floor and I nibbled at the bagels as I asked them how their breaks had been. They told me about their television sitcom like family Fourth of July celebrations, where everyone is included in their own way and everybody gets along even when they don't. Families where tolerance and love are the underlying themes. Unless you were watching MARRIED WITH CHILDREN; but even they seemed to get along really well and have a sense of family my own never managed to muster except for guests and strangers.

Gail's parents had taken her to a lake resort where she spent the time flirting with the water ski instructor to no avail, but it was just for fun because she was really in love with Jeff... Sharon had been to a string of restaurants and apparently went shopping every single day. Not sure if it was post-drinking brain cell damage or being tired or trying not to think about what I couldn't help thinking about or just the surrealism of their families compared to mine or the hyperrealism of their holidays compared to mine; but I had a hard time really listening to the details of what they were saying. I made sounds to emphasise how interesting I thought what they were saying was. I could take cues from them because they hadn't caught up the day before so I mimicked Gail's reactions to Sharon and vice versa and they didn't seem to notice.

As Sharon was describing the decor at her favourite mall and about to describe in detail a dress she bought - making moves to get up to retrieve it - there was knocking on the door and Antra came in; without me actually welcoming her to come into my room, while I was sitting in my pyjamas on the floor looking like Death's puke and feeling like Death's diarrhoea. Antra, of course, looked perky and cute like she always did, but had an especially strong air of contentedness about her. She tried to ask me how my break had been so I asked her if her earrings were new as I didn't think I'd seen them before and they really look great on you! I didn't think this actually. I thought they looked like the cheap trash often sold at accessories shops in malls and she normally wore much nicer jewellery than that, but I had sounded enthusiastic enough. Antra blushed a bit and swivelled on her left foot while hunching forward a bit. If she were six it would've been a good Shirley Temple impression. As she wasn't six I thought to myself 'Jesus H. mother-fucking tap-dancing Christ how can a person our age not be even the little bit of self-aware that's required to not behave like a 1930's cartoon character'. I think I was perhaps still a wee bit hungover after all despite the marathon sleep-in, bagels and peanut butter.

However, Sharon's face lit up when she saw Antra do her contortion. She smiled as she said "Ooohhh Antra, I can tell you have something special to tell about what you did over your holiday. Come on now, share with the class!" I looked down to pick at the bagel crumbs on my plate and was deciding to have another when Antra said "I hooked up with David! The earrings are a gift from him!"

I coughed as I choked on dry bread and turned my back on them as I leaned toward the mini-fridge to get a bottle of apple juice and made sure my reflection wasn't visible anywhere for them to see. Gail asked if I was ok and I hmmm'd in an affirmative way. Then as cool as I could muster, like I was asking what time the local cinema was showing a subtitled film I wasn't the least bit interested in seeing, I said "David? The David we eat with?" Hoping that if there was any trace of emotion in my voice it might be disguised as post coughing fit throatiness.

"Of course David, what other David would I be talking about?" Antra pouted.

Gail said "WELL!! This is news to us, so you're going to have to tell us EVERYTHING!"

Antra was delighted and plopped down between Gail and Sharon opposite me. I turned back and said they should spread out it was too cramped for four of us to sit on that space on the floor. I said my legs had started to fall asleep already from sitting Indian style. I feigned tingling legs and aching as I climbed up to my bunk; saying my body still really ached anyway so I'd be a better audience lying down. This actually wasn't true either. Now that I'd slept and eaten and had three horse strength ibuprofens my body felt ok. It was me. My soul if you believe in one or my consciousness if you want to argue philosophy. I felt like a worthless gaping waste of space where even mould wouldn't want to grow. I avoided looking at them until I was lying on my side with my plate and drink next to my stomach and able to lean back at any moment to sip if I needed to hide. From where I perched over them I could see inside the neckline of Antra's low cut button-front shirt and see she was wearing a fancy lace bra. Just like I do and just the kind David professed to love.

Antra said the night at the red house she'd thought he was attractive but he'd spent so much time with Becky she'd thought they were an item. Buuut when we'd all gone on the scavenger hunt and they were sent off together to get a bar stool he'd explained Becky was just a friend he grew up with; like Cherie, Randy and Dom (she looked up toward me and I grinned down), and that he was absolutely untied. I leaned back to lie my head on the pillow and look up at the ceiling. I was laying in the bed I'd "lost" my virginity in, to him. I'd given it freely I knew that. But she was talking about something that happened a few hours before David had quite seriously told me I was his ALL. On that same scavenger hunt night Antra was talking about David, and I had had sex (amazing incredible sex) and slept together in his mother's trailer, and he'd said with utmost sincerity that he loved me and I hadn't imagined that could be just talk. He'd said he loved me after we'd already been sleeping together for months. What was the point of that if it wasn't true? I'd already put out? But he'd told her he had no attachments.

I didn't know how to process this. I couldn't understand what was the motivation to lie to me? Could I be his ALL and him still feel absolutely untied? David and I were from different worlds. It was true his mother's group of people took sex very casually, but he'd been basically living with me for months before telling me he loved me and that same night hours earlier he'd told Antra he was absolutely untied. I realised my thoughts were looping and I was missing parts of what she was saying so I held my breath and just lay there listening.

Well, Antra and David had started having coffees together every morning after the spring break. They met in the student union coffee shop and talked for hours between classes and she thought his acting exercises were super interesting so he'd tell her all about them. Then she helped him with one, and then with another. Well, she'd given him some ideas and he liked them and said they'd been a great help. Here I thought to myself 'no wonder – he hasn't got a single original creative thought in his head', but in a doting sort of way as I'd thought it was charming he was so clueless about this aspect of himself.

Antra carried on, telling us she and David decided to meet up over the summer break so she could help him rehearse for some auditions. When she'd gone to his place they really just spent the whole time in his room getting frisky. Sharon wanted more details. Gail asked what did frisky mean? Antra blushed and said that it was really just a lot of kissing and heavy petting until the 4th of July. Gail prodded "ooohhh, what happened on the 4th of July Antra?" He had gone up to where she lived on the 4th of July to go to a hotel party with her friends from high school and, well, they had the room he booked alone all to themselves all night. After a few beats she whispered she'd given him a blow job. "What? The balcony didn't hear that?" I chirped.

Gail squealed somewhere between amusement and surprise "Antra gave David a BLOW JOB!" Sharon said "He must've thought it was the best fireworks ever!" I couldn't see their faces because I was still looking at the ceiling, but it felt like they MUST be grinning. Then Antra said it was awful. I rolled onto my side to peer over the edge with one eye and saw Antra had turned cherry red all over her face and was stricken by the jubilant reactions from Gail and Sharon. She'd never done it before but the whole time she'd felt like she was going to gag and he'd smelled like grain alcohol; which made her stomach turn even more, but he'd kept pushing her head down making it worse.

I rolled back onto my back but couldn't pinpoint what about that description of her 4th of July upset me most. I might as well have been an anime character when the screen goes black and all around her disappears except for the glass that can be heard breaking in the background. I guess it's meant to represent the character's emotions shattering into a bazillion shards. Or maybe their world-shattering, or maybe their beliefs. Anyone of those possibilities suited me as all three aspects of my reality were destroyed on hearing Antra go on. I had thought the diseases had to have come from Becky, but if he'd carried on with her too it might just as easily have been another girl. I wondered if Antra could have gonorrhoea or chancroid in her throat. I would have to look that up but it was for David to break it to her; wasn't it?

Gail said "how does it not surprise me he's a head pusher?" Then I heard Antra harrumph. Sharon asked "pushing your head down is shitty, but at least did he return the favour?" Antra didn't know what she meant. "What do you mean you don't know what I mean?" Sharon insisted. Antra apparently really didn't so Sharon asked did he go down on her or was she just too shy to talk about that? Antra said no; they'd just spooned after that. But not too long because it was before midnight and at midnight they'd gone out to party with the group and then they'd stayed up until breakfast. After breakfast he'd had to leave ASAP to go to be in time for the start of a trip his family did every year but that he hadn't really told her too much about, and she'd not really seen him too much after that. That was their annual camping trip to Yellowstone. I knew that but she didn't?

I realised I was clenching my fists when I felt my hands getting wet. I thought the juice bottle was leaking and crouched up to look for it and its cap when I saw the bottoms of my palms were red. I'd cut into them with my nails and I was bleeding more than a bit, but I didn't say anything because I wanted to hear the rest. I wrapped my palms in the corners of my top sheet and lay back down.

"Soooo, is that where you were last night? With him?" asked Sharon.

"Yes, but we didn't do anything because his roommate was there. We just watched TV until we fell asleep. Still it was nice. It was something else to wake up on a guy's dorm too. I had to do the walk of shame back to here before I could brush my teeth or my hair." That was Antra's first day back from the holiday break. She'd spent the night with David with his roommate there – so no hiding Antra – and they'd slept through the night together. I thought about this and thought all those reasons he'd never explicitly given but I'd understood in my rationalizations as to why couldn't stay the night through with me were probably all crap. He probably just snuck out like a thief to hide the embarrassment of being seen lowering himself to doing anything physical with me. I must've been some sort of consolation prise when he couldn't get any anywhere else.

Antra said "Anyway, that's enough about me. Cherie, how was your break?"

"Oh," I said "Didn't really do much of anything aside from watch TV and stuff around the house. My parents are very needy and don't like to let me out of their sight when I'm home."

"Oh I know what you mean!" Antra replied. "I had the hardest time shopping because every time I wanted to get something for myself my mom wanted to get it for me! No autonomy at all."

"I had that same problem" chimed Sharon. "It's like they feel withdrawal from not managing my every move. Oh, that reminds me I was going to show you my dress!" She got up to go get it and when she did she glanced over to me and gasped. "Cherie! You're bleeding!"

"I am? Oh, I guess I am a teeny bit. Hmmm, I must've hurt myself last night without realising."

"What are you on about? You've been sitting with us for over an hour and I've watched you schmear your bagels and you were fine." Sharon replied.

"I don't know" I whined and flopped over. "I don't feel well. I don't know what I'm doing. I think I'm still hung over."

"That'll teach you for getting blind stinking drunk without us!" said Gail. "Come on, let's go to our room and leave the damaged one to rest." She couldn't have been more on the money.

"Don't forget to come get me for dinner, pleeeaaase." I said.

"Of course not" Antra said. And they walked out. And I lay there while my mind whirred. I didn't move at all for about 90 minutes while I replayed Antra's juicy tale and overlaid her timeline with my own. What an idiot I'd been. If at all David had only been exclusive to me for a few months? If that? Who was I kidding he hadn't ever been. The evidence between Antra and the source of the STDs meant I could no longer believe that he had ever been just with me at any point. But it was hard to let go of that hope that I hadn't been a total chump. I kept wanting to believe that when David had said he loved me he must've meant it, but the evidence was to the contrary. Maybe his definition of love wasn't the standard dictionary definition. When my mind wasn't looping through feelings of betrayal, trying to solve the equation of how someone could do to another human being what David had done to me; it was just blank. I was like a TV showing static when the looping illogic was too much.

After about 90 minutes I got down from my bunk and went to take a shower. I kept forgetting which parts of myself I'd already washed and probably ended up doing everything several times over because someone coming into the room said "are you ok in there? You've been in the shower for over an hour. Not that it's a problem but just want to know you're ok?" It sounded like the resident assistant but I wasn't sure. I said yes, apologised and rinsed off. Then I sat in my robe on the bottom bunk in my room staring at the wall and whirring until Gail knocked on the door and asked if I was ready to go eat dinner. I told them I'd follow them down as I just needed to throw some clothes on. My hair had air dried by now so I shook myself alert and went down as quickly as I could. By the time I got there they were eating desserts but they were fine to wait for me to finish my own food.

I was supposed to eat lunch with Dom and Randy the next day in a cafeteria near the campus. They had told David and he had apparently told Antra, who told Sharon and Gail, so it was the full group sitting down together. When I saw David approaching I lost my breath. I was taken all over again by how attractive he was. I had really missed him but I wasn't allowed to miss him after what he'd done. I thought I might start screaming if I saw him touch Antra in front of me; or crying if my mind wandered. I made an excuse so I could get out of there. I had no idea if anyone bought what I was saying but I'd been acting oddly for a couple of days so Sharon and Gail didn't question my leaving without having eaten anything.

I was looking at David as I feigned my excuse and saw him make a face that, if I hadn't known better by this point in time I would have thought was disappointment. He actually followed me out of the cafeteria into the hallway. I was amazed by this public display of interest in my person but kept walking toward the door to the outside. He caught up to me and grabbed my upper arm to make me stop. I was annoyed by this. I said "what the fuck David?" He said "Cherie, what's going on? I've really missed you. Where were you yesterday?" I asked if he'd missed me while he slept with Antra in his bed, or if he'd missed me while she was blowing him on the fourth of July. He just stood there looking stunned. I tried to wrench my arm free but he was gripping really tightly.

I asked if he hadn't gotten the message that I called in July? He said it really wasn't cool to call his mother's house; especially given the wild accusations I made, but yes he'd gotten the message. "And?" I demanded. And he'd been treated and he was fine now. "Ha! So not wild accusations then; but important information" I said. He said yes, I was right and he was sorry. He hadn't realised it was gonorrhoea and chancroid. He'd had chlamydia a few times and had thought it was that and possibly warts doing something strange as they showed symptoms at the same time. He hadn't appreciated he'd gotten something else. But I didn't need to call his mother as he'd gone to a clinic on his own when he saw he was developing symptoms. I made a mental note he'd gone to a clinic before I'd called him, but he hadn't thought to call me or let me know I might have STDs. He'd said it casually; he'd had chlamydia a few times, like it was a common cold. He'd thought he might have warts; like it was acne. An abrupt panic gripped me that I might have other infections, but passed quickly as I remembered Dr. Glenda had run the full spectrum of available tests just to be on the safe side. Still, my heart was pounding from indignation and adrenaline. How could he possibly think it was no big deal? Or did he think I was so stupid and naïve that he might make me believe it was no big deal? Maybe he thought I was that easy to manipulate. It was true his opinion had been of primary importance to me since the day we'd met. On this matter though; I had a medical opinion that allowed me to reality check David's unconcerned manner. STDs are anything but inconsequential.

Even after having had nearly two months to think of nothing else and to convince myself David was a mammoth bastard; which I hadn't yet managed to totally do, I was astounded at what he said. He had been fully aware he was likely giving me STDs; he'd just thought they were different ones. I remembered a campus leaflet that said knowingly having sex without disclosing STDs was a form of rape. I said as much to him. He said "Jesus Cherie, it's not like I have AIDS. All you needed was some antibiotics." I was enraged he could be so laidback about it. He definitely saw nothing at all wrong with what he'd done.

People kept walking by and bumping into us. I was afraid someone we knew might come out of the cafeteria and hear what we were arguing about, but I wasn't about to just let this drop. I wasn't sure I might ever have another chance to speak with him about it and I wanted him to know my mind. I was trying to whisper and shout at the same time as I said "How the fuck did you get them in the first place? When did you even have the TIME to sleep with someone else to get diseases that you knew you might give me when you were having sex with me? Was it Becky? Were you sleeping with her in the hours you weren't with me? What?" His face had gone hard. He pushed me by the arm he still had in a vice grip until we were up against the wall and out of the way of other people walking through. He said "Listen Cherie; don't pretend this is something it isn't. I never forced you to do anything." "No, you're right, you didn't. But you did make me believe you cared about me when you obviously don't."

His face softened and he looked hurt now. "Cherie, how can you say that? I love you sweetheart." He tried to kiss me but I moved my face to look away. I didn't know what else to do. It didn't compute. How could that be? I was looking away when I asked "if you love me then what was Antra doing giving you a blowjob on July 4th? Why is she wearing jewellery you gave her?" He said he couldn't control what Antra did but he hadn't invited her to do it. He'd been really drunk and not entirely aware of what was going on. He'd thought he was dreaming when she started it but then he was caught up. The jewellery was payment for her helping him with his rehearsals. It had actually been agreed between them before the first day she'd started doing that. He couldn't help it if she pretended it was a gift. I didn't know if it was possible what he was saying. Could she have started doing that to him while he was asleep or incapacitated? If he were really that drunk wouldn't that have made it nigh impossible for her to get a physical response out of him? Of course, I'd never really liked Antra in the first place, so it was convenient that his reply put her in a bad light. "But," I said, "then what was she doing sleeping in your dorm room the other night?" He said all they'd done was watch TV; where was the harm in that? He felt sorry for her because she seemed to be lonely.

I was trying to sustain my anger but having him up close to me, whispering in my ear; pushed up close against me with my back against the wall, I was weakening. I feel his warm breath on my neck and I could smell his hair. I wanted so badly to believe he loved me and everything else was a mistake or misunderstanding. I think he could tell because his grip loosened a bit and he put his other hand on my chin to pull my head around to look at him. I hadn't wanted him to see the pain in my face, but there was no avoiding it now. I said "but she said when we were all doing the scavenger hunt you told her you were completely unattached." "Really? Why should I tell her who I go out with Cherie? Come on, I thought you liked us being private. It means it's just us with no meddling." His eyes were so amazingly blue and striking, and they seemed to be expressing pleading concern.

I steeled myself. I made myself think about the miscarriage. I didn't want to tell him though. If he was telling me the truth it would probably only hurt him needlessly. If he was lying he probably wouldn't give a shit. I wanted to believe he was telling the truth but honestly, he had become such a good actor it was tricky to know for sure. Some people are just world-class liars. Terrorists' families often come out saying they would never have guessed what their son/brother/husband had been plotting. David had told me loads of stories that proved he (like me) often lived an external life or reality that was quite different from what he thought or felt within. I wanted to believe him about Antra even though I would never lose my right to be outraged by the diseases he gave me. I was desperate to let myself trust what he was saying. Despite everything, I still loved him. How could I not? If I had wished a person into being he couldn't have been a better intellectual match or more handsome to me than David was. But what he'd done was unforgivable wasn't it? The sight of him; in spite of all that had happened, inspired a sort of Greek chorus to repeat without cessation in my brain 'I love you. I love you. I love you.' The chorus wouldn't shut up. Maybe it was a pavlovian response, but it was strong and unquestionable. I wanted to hate him but I was still in love. I struggled hard to keep to the point of our conversation.

I said "How is it just us David? Who did you get the STDs from then? Because I've never slept with anyone but you and you know it." Now his face was all affection and sorrow. He said "I can't lie to you Cherie. Remember when you had the flu and just lay in bed and didn't want me to come round?" I nodded; I'd had a 103° fever and spent several days semiconscious. I don't like for people to see me when I'm ill and had made sure he stayed away. The thought he might see me with dripping snot or snot encrusted on my nose or with puffy eyes was horrific; let alone the potential smell of illness. "Well, Becky and I went out and started reminiscing and well, I'm not proud of what I did. I got carried away. Of course, I didn't tell you because I was afraid of how you might react."

I was vexed again. He was afraid of how I might react? He was only coming clean with me on all this now because he'd been caught. If I hadn't been damaged by his sleeping around I'd be none the wiser. And his feelings were apparently so shallow that a day or two without me was all it took for him to have sex with someone else? Or was I supposed to think his sex drive was so strong he couldn't go without sex no matter who was in front of him? Didn't that mean that the sex between us was meaningless as well? I wondered how many other girls there had been between Antra and the return to campus that I might never know about. I said "David, how do you want me to react? You gave me diseases because you weren't honest with me. I suppose I'm lucky they weren't incurable." He grunt-sighed heavily like I was being unreasonable. I looked at him and was overcome by the desire to put my arms around him and hug him close. He looked desolately sad and I wanted to ease his pain. Then I remembered I was the injured party here and tried to make myself angry again. But in such close proximity to him it was very challenging to think straight. I could only do that if I didn't let my heart take over. I asked him "how many others did you have sex with over the summer?" He said I didn't want to know the answer to that. I said "Oh yes I do. I really very much want to know. I think I need to know." He said "Forget them Cherie. They don't matter." "They absolutely matter if they are potentially going to make me sick again." He let go my arm and took a step backward.

Randy had come into the hallway. David must've seen Randy's reflection in the window behind me. Randy remarked on the fact that we were both still there in the hall. He would've seen us standing close together, but not abnormally close given we were on the opposite side of a constant stream of people going in and out of the building. David was nonchalant saying we'd gotten wrapped up in discussion about whether we should go to the Irish bar or try somewhere new. Randy voted for a change and looked at me enquiringly. I said I didn't care; but I had to go as I was really late for class now. I walked past David without looking at him. I focused on the doors to the outside until I was through them. David let me walk away this time.

When I was outside I let go a grunting scream that made a couple of people nearby turn their heads, but I didn't care and kept walking. In my head, that was it. It was evident David had been with more than just Becky and Antra. It was clear he wouldn't come clean about it. It was plain that he didn't think it was my business to know who he'd been with or how often. He apparently thought I should be happy to share him with an undisclosed number of women about who I was not allowed to know any detail. The ones I did know about were women I didn't like as people. The thought of doing anything physical with Becky made my skin crawl. Far be it from me to judge what she did when it was her choice, but to me her choices were disgustingly repulsive. Her attitude to sex made it a sort of exploratory sport, whereas, for me it was an incredibly private, personal and intimate act. By sleeping with Becky, David had effectively made me sleep with her and my skin just would not stop crawling now that the thought had crossed my mind. He'd given me her diseases. Antra was repugnant to me as well; although, for different reasons. Antra was just an infant.

This all made me realise I couldn't actually know the real David or I would understand the attraction those girls held for him. He couldn't possibly care about my thoughts or feelings or he would have understood it was impossible for me to accept him being with them while he was with me. His expressions of love for me were lies.

During the summer, when I was thirteen I tried to run away from my parents' house. It had been a hot summer of being cooped up in a house where I was made to feel an unwanted intruder. I didn't know anyone in the neighbourhood; but even if I had I wasn't allowed to venture into the front yard (or anywhere else for that matter), and I had no means of transport anyway. I'd been made to sit still indoors for weeks. There was a limit to how much TV a kid could watch. TV, books and music were really my only company since my mother slept all day. She only got up in time to get ready when my father was coming home from work. One day I was knocked around because I hadn't been smiling when I came to sit down to breakfast. I'd spent most of the rest of that day in my room listening to music.

In the evening I was lying on the floor in my room with my head facing the speakers of my boom box, listening to Blue Monday by New Order, and didn't hear the parents yell for me to go to the table. I was still singing along with the music when I was pulled up off the floor by my ponytail. My father was screaming at me for not having headed him when he called. I was wobbly because he didn't give me time to stand up before he started punching and kicking me; all the while screaming who the hell did I think I was? When he said move I should immediately jump. I made the mistake of saying I hadn't heard him because I was listening to my tape. He pushed me away from him with force. I hit the wall so hard my head made a crack sound. As I started to slump, he picked up the boom box and then bashed it against the footboard of my bed. He damaged the bed as well as the box, but it was still making sound so he pulled the tape out and broke it in two. Then he turned back to me and hit me repeatedly while saying I had no right to avoid them by staying in my room. I must sit downstairs and do whatever my mother needed whenever she asked. Then he pulled me by the hair all the way to the table in the kitchen. When I was finally allowed to go back to my room when they were going to bed, I saw there was a mark in the paint on the wall where my head had hit it. The boom box was ruined. I didn't give a shit about the bed; it was a relic and the mattress was crap anyway.

The next day after screaming at for not smiling when I came down to breakfast, my father left without hitting me because he was running late. My mother was back in bed five minutes later. She basically waited to see his car had gone down round the corner out of sight and left the cleaning up for me to do. I didn't do it though. I was still pissed off about my boom box and the irrationality of my father's temper tantrums. I was fed up with my imprisonment. I wanted it all to end. I thought about packing a bag but there was really no point as nothing I owned was mine. Everything I had belonged to my father; he'd made that plenty clear pretty much every day I was there. So with the clothes on my back and about twenty dollars I'd squirrelled away by not buying drinks at school lunches before the summer break; I walked out the front door.

It was a glorious sunny day. As I walked down the street I heard birds chirping. A cat followed me for a while then went back home. I kept walking right on out of the neighbourhood and toward town. By the time I made it to the bus station it was nearly 11 am. That's how rural the place was. At the bus station the woman behind the counter refused to sell me a ticket. She said twenty dollars might get me as far as Chicago, but what did I think I was going to do there? I said I didn't care. Anything would be better than the life I had. The woman was supercilious with me. She asked if I had been denied the top of the range must have bike, or if my mother had refused to buy me some fancy label dress or something. I said I didn't have any bike and my clothes were all from a second-hand store. She didn't know me or my life and she should just do her job and sell me a ticket. Then she changed tact. She asked me what would I do for money once I'd spent my twenty dollars? I hadn't thought about that. I'd figure it out when I was on the other side. I bet I could work at a fast food place at the very least. I didn't think you even needed to know how to read to work at those places. She looked down her nose and said I was too young. Didn't I know the law prohibits child labour? I'd either end up begging or turning tricks by the end of the week. I thought about the after school specials I seen about streetwise teens and honcho gangs. I told her I thought I could handle it. Then she said she'd tried the nice way but she couldn't let me go. She could either drive me home on her lunch break or I could walk home, but I wasn't getting a bus ticket out of her.

The powerlessness to change my life overwhelmed me. I asked her if she couldn't see my black eye. The ticket seller said "Honey, what do I know how you got that?" When she did drive me home she was at least nice enough not to come to the door with me. She just watched from the street to make sure I went inside. She must've gotten an eyeful of my mother smacking me while yelling why the hell weren't the dishes done and why was I getting her out of bed. I never saw or heard from the ticket lady again, but the futility of that attempt stayed with me. For years after, every time I wanted to run I remembered I didn't have any means. I had to wait until circumstances changed. Meantime I gritted my teeth. Every single day – for years.

The next evening the whole group went out together to (you guessed it) the Irish bar. I tried to avoid looking at David but it was pointless.

I was ferromagnetised to him. He seemed not to have any cares in the world. He was smiling and laughing in conversation with many; among them Antra and Becky. I was dying inside. I felt like this was some kind of test, but I wasn't solving it; I was just a piece of the puzzle. I felt like a block of green wood being forced into a space meant for a red rubber ball. I couldn't let on I was really just a block of greenwood. I tried singing along with the lyrics but kept getting distracted. I tried playing darts but I couldn't keep track of the numbers I was meant to be hitting. I went to stand next to Dom. The whole time I was standing around listening to others talk I was thinking 'How could he do it? How can he stand there with them? Why has he done this to me? Why is he still doing this to me?' Dom saw I was out of it and told me so. I said I might be coming down with something and went back to the dorms. It was a relief to not have to see David any longer, or wonder whether I was managing to keep it together outwardly. Luckily the way back to my dorm room was ingrained in my subconscious because I was crying and couldn't really see where I was going, but I made it back physically unscathed.

About an hour later I was lying in bed. I was still using the top bunk even though I was still happily sharing my room with an absent Jessica. I'd gotten used to it I suppose, and had made up the lower bunk like a sofa. Tears were streaming down my cheeks but I was quiet and I had no problem hearing the knock on my door. I got down and opened it to see David. I hadn't expected him. It seemed out of the blue and I was a little bit in shock at the sight of him. I'd thought after our last argument it was unequivocally over because he had no remorse about sleeping around and I'd been frank about that not being acceptable to me. I'd thought it was explicitly over because he'd shown me no mercy at all earlier that night, given he knew full well how I felt about the women he'd spent his time with in front of everyone. There's no way he didn't know how it all affected me. We'd just discussed it the previous day.

David's face was all concern but he didn't say anything. Looking at him my bloody Greek chorus was on again saying 'I LOVE YOU' in my head but I was entirely certain now he didn't care what I felt. His actions proved my feelings were immaterial to him. Tears started flowing again and all strength left my body. How could he have spent the hours cheerily chatting away with Becky and Antra. How could he sleep with them? How could he make me watch him laughing and drinking with two women he'd betrayed me with and then just show up here? How could he knowingly give me STDs? How could he pretend he loved me so convincingly for so long; when the facts and his actions revealed he couldn't possibly? Everything must just have been some perverse act. My emotional turmoil was a Terry Gilliam movie.

I was so drained I couldn't even sob. The tears just kept streaming down. David leaned forward to kiss me and I just stood there immobilised by my anguish. He knew full well how I felt and yet he'd spent the evening talking to the two people who were the axis of my heartache. As he kissed me I wasn't kissing him back but I was too exhausted to react. He pushed his way into the room, making me step backward as he came in. He closed the door behind him and locked it. Something disturbed me when I saw him do that. I had a flashback to the first night he'd come inside and closed the door behind him. I had been so happy that day. The two nights were Yin and Yang. I started mumbling "How could you do it? Why?" but I don't think he heard me.

David carried on kissing me as he undid my pyjama top. I wasn't kissing him back. I was saying "No, no. Please David. No," but I was limp and tired. I'm not sure how loudly I was managing to say it. I didn't push him off or fight him because I was feeble; consumed by hopelessness. He didn't love me. I didn't believe anything about what he made me feel anymore except for the pain and deception. I couldn't believe anything he'd said to me about how he felt. His duplicity made me tell my instincts and my Greek Chorus to shut up. He didn't love me. I wasn't sure what was going on but I didn't want his contaminated skin to touch me. I felt so hollow and weak I thought my being might just wink out of existence if he kept touching me. None of this meant anything to him. It felt like my whole body was made up of nothing but sorrowful weeping and I hoped I might dissolve into a puddle that gravity could drain away.

I just stood there crying and whining softly over and over "no, please no" as David maneuvered me onto the lower bunk. He was saying "Cherie, I love you" while I lay there like a rag doll crying silently. How could he keep saying that when it wasn't true? How could he lie so easily about something so important? As he fucked me I felt detached from myself, like I wasn't there. I wondered what Antra and Becky looked like when they were with him. I wondered if he made the same faces with them as with me. Then pictures from Dr. Cooper's big book of STDs flashed through my head. When he came he opened his eyes and looked me in the face. He seemed to only just notice in that moment I was crying. I was despondent and feeling wretched. He cared so little about how I felt he hadn't even noticed that I hadn't moved at all. He hadn't headed my refusals. Who I was or what I wanted didn't seem to matter at all. I was ostensibly just a hole no matter what he said. I wished that by wishing I might pass out or die so I wouldn't have to suffer through another minute. I managed to turn onto my side to look at the wall and I covered my face. He hugged me from the back and whispered "Cherie, honey, don't you understand? I love **you**." At that I croaked "No you don't. You don't give a shit about me."

It was hard to speak intelligibly. I had to breathe deep and concentrate to say "If you did you would've come here to talk to me; to discuss things. You wouldn't have spent the night cozied up to Antra and Becky. You wouldn't have ..." I couldn't say it. I nearly choked as I accidentally breathed in spittle and tears that had run down my cheek into my mouth. He sighed heavily and said he wished he could use the Ipcress machine on me to make me forget them. I thought I wouldn't have to if he hadn't had sex with them; but I only managed to say "why are you debasing me like this?"

I looked over my shoulder and saw his face was just confused. I honestly don't think he understood what he'd done to me. I thought again about telling him about the miscarriage, but didn't think it should change anything between us. I decided he couldn't possibly care so I kept it to myself. I didn't need his pity on top of everything else, and I didn't want him to think I was trying to manipulate him. But thinking about that -on top of the ruinous violation I was already feeling- made the torture visible on my face again and when he saw it he stood up and got dressed. He didn't say anything else. He just left.

After that I told Randy and Dom I'd had a falling out with David but didn't tell them why or what over. Dom probably thought I was just jealous. Randy didn't care because it wasn't his drama. They did manage to keep him away from lunch after that, and he generally stayed away from our weekend nights out. The time in between was long and lonely; despite Sharon and Gail's efforts to keep me cheery.

The last time Antra ate with us she told us she was over the moon because she and David were officially an item. David had told her she was the first girl to really totally get him. It's not that we did anything to make Antra stop coming; it's that after that, she apparently hung on his arm 24/7. She couldn't be bothered with us any longer. I was glad to be rid of the stress of having to pretend her being around didn't make me want to vomit. Could it be possible Antra was happy for David to sleep around? I highly doubted she knew but it was not my problem.

I didn't say anything at all but Sharon and Gail weren't stupid. They'd already noticed David wasn't joining us at lunches anymore. I don't suppose they thought we'd ever been an item but they understood David and I were no longer friends. It wasn't important to them because they'd never been that close to him. David became a taboo subject, then a non-subject, and eventually by not seeing him and not hearing about him the torment died down.

The semester dragged on because the classwork was no more engaging than the first year's had been. I tried to distract myself with an art class and that worked while I was busy on a sketch. I would forget about everything except what I was drawing and that suited me fine. I know I wasn't very good at it but it was therapeutic. I spent most of that semester trying not to think. When I found myself thinking too much I'd get the paper and charcoal and focus on what I saw until everything else dropped away to nothingness.

Occasionally Randy would forget our unspoken exclusion and mention David was doing something with this girl or that. He'd say Antra was clueless. I'd mentally note David hadn't amended his behaviour and then I'd remind Randy I didn't care what David got up to. I might have been too convincing on that point.

In the spring semester David and Antra started coming back to our weekend evenings. Maybe he was bored with her company by now? He must've thought I was over it, but I wasn't. Seeing him chatting nonchalantly to any girl at all made me wonder what else he did with her. Did he tell them he loved them? Would she get a disease or would he spare her? Did Antra think he was exclusive with her? Did he care if she ever said no? Did she have any idea at all of what had happened between us? After a couple of weeks of staying on the other side of the bar, one Friday David approached me to try to start a conversation. I couldn't even be civil to him. I just turned around and went home.

I decided I needed something else to do with my weekends. I didn't want to spend any more days risking proximity to David because it was too distressing. The nights I had seen him I'd lost sleep as I relived the betrayal in my mind over and over while lying in bed alone in my room. No matter how many times I went over it I could never understand how I could care so much about a person who cared so little about me or my wellbeing. He had taken my perdition in his stride. No amount of movies, TV or literature could have prepared me for it. Every time I started thinking about it I'd get depressed and stuck in a rut. I couldn't put enough distance between us to avoid being reminded again.

I auditioned to sing in a local band and they chose me. From there on I spent most of my time with crunchy hippie types that didn't shower often enough and only talked about music and other bands or the gigs we were going to do. It was a good distraction, probably precisely because we did not really have anything in common, aside from the music. The band was called the JIMJAMS and consisted of drums, bass, guitar and myself. They'd been playing together for about three years and their music was original, as in it wasn't a cover band even though it wasn't genius either. I suppose we sounded something like if Melissa Etheridge was fronting the Divinyls. They even let me use some of my own poetry as lyrics from time to time. It was like starting a completely new existence with no history. I let myself be creative with my makeup and dress. I cut all my hair off and hung feathers from my earlobes. Come to think of it, I wasn't that innovative. I probably looked like an extra from an Adam Ant video, but it was not a common look on my university campus. It made me feel better because when I looked in the mirror, I did not see the loser who'd let herself be fooled and broken. I saw a free character that was living each day as it came and not thinking about the past or the future.

My friends were still my friends, but I saw a lot less of them and we shared less given we didn't spend nearly so much time together as before. Randy and Dom came by once in a while to see me sing and we still caught up every week, but I never went specifically with them to parties or bars anymore. Gail and Sharon still ate dinner with me every weekday. They actually tried a few times to set me up with men but stopped because I refused to go on any dates.

In my third year, I did start to date some guys I met while I was doing gigs with the JIMJAMS. I tried going out with quite a few guys, refusing to judge anyone who asked me out until we'd had a proper conversation, no matter how weird or unappealing they might seem. This confused the guys in the band because I didn't seem to have a type, but I had up front refused to do anything physical with them the day I auditioned. I don't know if they thought that was funny or professional. They probably thought it was smart to accept since they'd had to audition a singer in the first place when the last one had broken up with the guitar player, Harry, for a bartender. Frankly, the thought my flesh touching the flesh of any of these guys made my flesh crawl. The drummer, Hugo, was an overweight pothead with whom it was nearly impossible to have a coherent conversation on any subject that didn't have to do with music, his poverty, getting toked or thoughts directly connected to one of those subjects. The bass player, Angel, was a smart guy but was also a vegan with halitosis and hygiene issues, no dress sense and very narrow interests. The guitarist, Harry, was, in fact, the hairiest guy I'd ever seen who wasn't wearing a costume and pretending to be a gorilla or yeti. The guys from the band were fine for my musical entertainment and distraction, but they were certainly not guys I would ever in a million years want to exchange bodily fluids with. I didn't ever say that to them, though; obviously. They were reliable colleagues as far as I was concerned. They treated me like one of the guys. That suited me fine.

My failed dates became a running joke with the JIMJAMS. I never really hit it off with a single one of the berks who asked me out. I never believed anything complimentary they said about me. I never let myself believe anything I might like about them could be true. I was inevitably proved right. Guys would show they were out of their depth in a discussion about something they vowed to be a fan of, or they displayed ignorance of key facts about issues they claimed were important to them. None of them was attractive enough to make up for the predictable disappointment their personalities caused. To me they were all just a bunch of immature assholes making anything up to get in a girl's pants. I didn't want to be that girl.

Well, but to be completely honest, I did succumb on two occasions. About a year after excluding David from my life I started being harassed by a bartender at one of the places the group played regularly. He was a slick ladies' man who clearly got a lot of action with girls who drank there and; of course, he wasn't WHOLLY offensive to the eyes. He just wasn't my type. He was too short, barrel-chested, too pug-nosed, too base and his body odour was akin to stale beer. It could be he simply wasn't hygienic. Anyway, he went on and on and on about how a body like mine shouldn't go to waste… I ignored him for a few months; which in actual days of contact was eight or ten given that bar was only one of several where the JIMJAMS played.

Then, for a film studies course, I saw a five hour-long Russian saga about how love drives people mad. It was a beautifully shot and painfully well-acted story of forbidden hidden love that is kyboshed by circumstance. I had never before cried watching a film because I normally couldn't even achieve suspension of disbelief, but by the end of this one I had used an entire packet of tissues. I was so affected by it I felt the dejection of a castaway adrift for aeons. I experienced a frantic deep loneliness that grew rapidly and was magnified exponentially on seeing any random couple smile happily at each other. So, when I ran into the bartender the next day he suddenly vaguely reminded me of David. I was so very intensely lonely I slept with a man that was inconsequential to my own emotions. He was just a warm body to take advantage of; which I supposed was what he habitually did with the girls that went by the bar. Unfortunately, he was rather inept in bed so after we had sex not only did I feel emptier than before due to having done it with the wrong person; I also felt like I'd been swindled by a guy who clearly didn't have a clue of how to please a female. He did in fact realise he'd underperformed and thereafter was always skittish around me when we went to the bar where he worked. I ended up having to always get the guys in the band buy my drinks because he wouldn't look me in the eye. After that I swore to myself never ever again. And no more Russian love stories or love stories of any kind. Thereafter I was an avid action movie fan.

But I did in fact have yet another regrettable lapse. It was at a party at the end of sophomore year. I was out with Randy and Dom and we did a bar crawl then ended up at someone's house. I had gotten smashed beyond belief because I was dreading an enduring summer being at home with my parents. There was a guy at the party that had the right kind of attitude and smile. I thought to myself 'what the hell, life is short'. To spare you the long version of this anecdote: almost as soon as we were getting undressed, I threw upon him. Needless to say nothing else happened that night? Maybe it does need saying. After I heaved the contents of my stomach onto the guy he ran to his bathroom screaming, "What the fuck? I can't believe you threw up on me!" I, momentarily alert from having reduced the alcohol content in my body; left his apartment while saying how sorry I was for vomiting but clearly, I needed to go home. I don't know if I ever saw that guy again because I don't remember his name, what he looked like or where he lived. I only remember the horrific sense of reprobation for having let myself get into that situation. After that I swore to myself never ever again. But this time really, NEVER again.

I was still a corporeal human being, though; a mammalian animal so to speak. I had already overcome the stigma of catholic education earlier that scholastic year by getting a Kegel, although the clerk at the drug store clearly wasn't over the stigma of anything connected with or relating to the vagina. When I asked for it he acted like I'd asked for porn. I convinced him (already having convinced myself) that I needed it for health purposes.

Before the Christmas break sophomore year I had ordered a rabbit by post from a catalogue I found in the dorm lounge. Over time through use of my toy, I learned how to dissociate my sentiments from my physical responses. It took discriminating rational effort and time; given for me any pleasurable sexual impression was directly tied to David. At first nothing but thinking of him inspired me to use the rabbit. I did finally manage it, though. Progressively I replaced thoughts of David with pure sensation.

The partition I achieved between body and mind made me a far lot pickier about who I'd go out with. After my Russian saga mistake; I never again felt any urge or need for physical satisfaction from men I wasn't absolutely attracted to. This was a tall order after having met and lost near flawlessness. Attraction required intellectual as well as visual characteristics to be met. The fact that David had ended up treating me poorly didn't detract from the fact that what I had felt was genuine, and; except for his wandering ways and disease-ridden dick, he was nigh perfect. My vow of never ever again -but REALLY- basically meant protracted celibacy; unless you count toys as sexual partners or define masturbation as sex. Personally, sex isn't sex if you're by yourself. Sexual pleasure does not equal sexual encounters.

Anyway, I avoided the emotional roller coaster my friends seemed to be taking turns on. For me, once had been enough for me to learn my lesson. I wasn't getting back on unless I was wholly convinced the man was absolutely worth the effort.

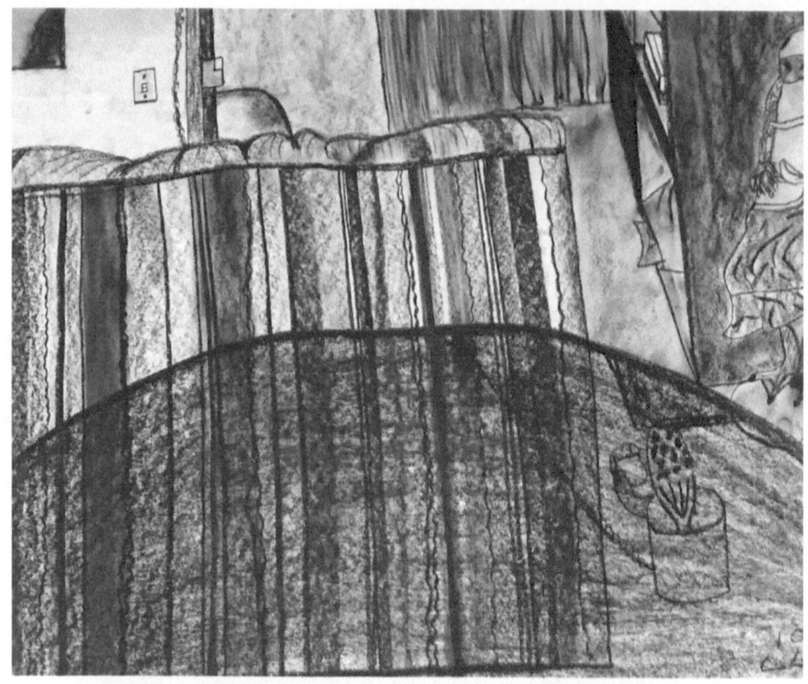

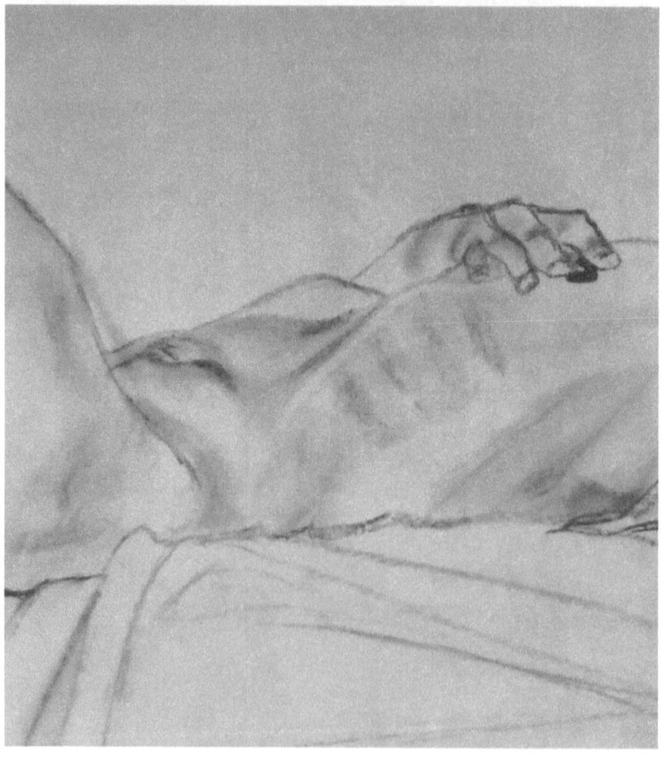

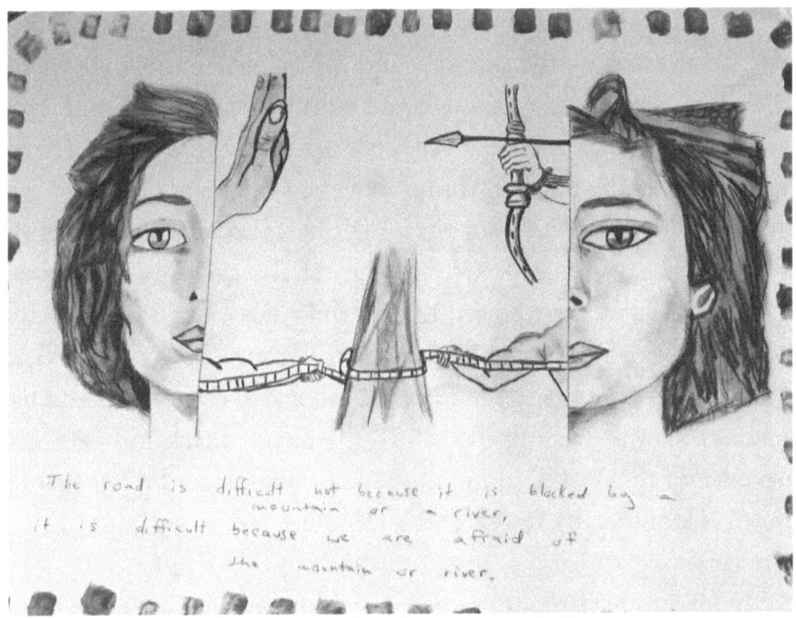

I got the scar over my right eye one day walking home from the gym. I was in one of my hopeful eras. I was interested in a guy I wanted to try dating, so gave a shit what I might look like to the opposite sex and decided it needed tightening up. I have never EVER worked out for the joy of it or to feel better or because it was healthy. My only motivation ever has been to make sure I look as good as possible within the limits of reality and without surgery, which I cannot afford, but I wouldn't know who to trust with a knife anyway.

Anyway, when I do go for it I commit and I spend minimum two hours a day between cardio machines and weight training and whatever else there may be. I avoid showering in the gym because I don't like being in close proximity with strangers who try to talk to you when you are naked. If there were a jacuzzi or a sauna I might've used that but I was strapped so was going to a cheap dive gym where policemen went to bulk up that was about ten blocks from my flat.

I was walking home with a skirt over my shorts, a floppy hat to hide my sweaty hair and in sandals because it was actually too hot to wear proper shoes. I was looking where I was going because there was construction work on the sidewalk and the signs kept moving every day as the work progressed, although the workers had gone home by the time I got there. An open top car came up behind me on the left with three guys in it all shouting things like "hey there girly"; "prissy missy with a hat" and "show us your tits". I felt harassed to be honest as I was just trying to get home quickly to shower. I turned to look at them because I thought I recognised one of the voices, but I couldn't really see their faces or recognise the car. Then I turned back to see where I was going as I remembered there had been a sign coming up and bang! My forehead was gushing blood as I'd walked smack into the razor-sharp edge of the post holding up the temporary sign. I'll bet that kind of post is forbidden by health and safety rules today but *sigh* this was before that.

My forehead started to gush so fast I lost sight in my right eye and I heard the guys in the car say things like "oh shit" "crap" and then the squealing of their tires as they drove off. In the corner of my blood free eye I pictured only a blur as they disappeared around the corner while I got a t-shirt out of my gym bag and held it against my forehead. From there I walked to the emergency room where I was told off for not being more careful where I go. What was wrong with me? Didn't I realise I could've lost an eye?

In the second semester of my third year in college I was enjoying a small amount of celebrity as the JIMJAMS started to get regular gigs at different bars around campus. Randy, Dom, Gail, Sharon and the rest of the group all started coming regularly to watch us perform. I suppose they liked being able to say they knew the chick in the band, or maybe they actually liked the music, or maybe they were just tired of the Irish bar and the Red House. Anyway, it had been about a year and a half since I had surgically removed David from my life and circle of people; and I had thought I was getting on well. Then one Saturday evening, I was taking a bow when I saw him standing next to Randy and Dom against the wall in the far corner of the bar. David popped into my vision out of nowhere like a rogue planet emerging from behind a cloud of dark matter. When I saw him my heart skipped several beats and my body temperature dropped. I knew instantly I was no more over him that night than I had been the evening, a year and a half earlier, when I had walked away from him without saying a word. I marvelled I had not seen him standing there earlier, but then thought he'd probably only just showed up when we'd finished our set.

David looked amazingly good; still a sharp dresser and still in fantastic shape. I wondered that on a university campus with tens of thousands of students in my age range; not a single other man I'd come across during my two and a half years there was even remotely as physically attractive as David. Perhaps his sheer existence on campus wielded an action at a distance on my own urges. Rather than properly thanking the audience I was standing there like a rabbit in headlights and David grinned when he saw I was unmistakably looking at him. Angel, the bass player, had to slap me on the shoulder to wake me from my reverie. Angel had been asking me to help him move the amp. I was relieved we had finished for the night. I probably wouldn't have been able to remember the words to anything after spotting David. I felt extremely lucky I hadn't seen David standing there during the set as I imagined myself doing a stunned bunny impression mid-verse. Then I supposed he surely wasn't there to see me. I concentrated on getting the gear put away; pushing and carrying things to the van.

The guys were considering whether to stay for a drink or call it a night when Hugo, the drummer, jerked his head toward me saying I had a fan to attend to. Harry smirked and Angel laughed as he said "I think this one's different." I turned around to see David standing a couple of feet behind me; patiently waiting for our conversation to wrap up. David waved and pointed to a fresh mug of beer he was holding up; then pointed to Randy and Dom who were standing by the bar. I turned back to the guys and Hugo said "Oh, you look panicked. Do you want to get into the van?" I honestly did want to get into the van. I wanted to run and hide in the dark and not have to come out for a very long time. I had the sensation my blood had abandoned my limbs. I couldn't believe David was there at all but couldn't grasp why he would want to talk to me, and wasn't sure I would be able to stand it if he did. Then Harry said Dom owed them a round and he wanted to cash it in. The guys all forgot about me as they made for the bar. Rather than stand there stupidly by myself next to the empty stage, or go home by myself without saying anything to my friends who'd stopped by; I walked behind the guys like a straggling child wondering whether I looked fat in my outfit or if my makeup had held up under the lights. I was abruptly mindful my bra straps were showing and their bright orange colour clashed with my outfit.

I couldn't remember ever having felt so self-conscious or insecure about my looks. Not even when in high school I'd idiotically worn a French bikini at the public swimming pool. Seconds later David was standing in front of me, blocking my path and handing me a beer. I wasn't sure what to do. I looked toward the bar for Dom and Randy but they were wrapped up in banter with the guys from the band. It pissed me off they could leave me exposed this way. Hadn't I made it very extremely clear to them how I felt about having to see David? I unhappily inferred it was too much to expect them to look out for me. I supposed they were engrossed in some argument about trivia. David had to see me looking past him when he asked if I didn't drink beer anymore. I said sure but how could I know what he would give me wasn't spiked? He looked nonplussed for a nanosecond. Then he was grinning again saying "what a card" in the cheesiest of all possible voices. I sighed and took it from him; and tried to move around him toward the bar again when he put his hand on my shoulder and asked me to sit down with him. Why not just talk for a bit; the two of us? I could think of plenty of reasons why not, but any one of them would have unambiguously revealed that I wasn't over him so I said "sure, why not?"

David told me he had missed me terribly. He couldn't understand what had happened to our friendship. I rolled my eyes and said "come on, really?" He said he was a huge fan of my group. He'd actually been to see us perform many times but he hadn't come up to say hello because he wasn't sure whether I'd welcome it. He'd done it this time because Randy had said 'what the hell'. In that moment I couldn't know the context of that statement from Randy; or whether it was true that he'd said it, but I damned Randy to burn in the lowest level inferno imaginable. I couldn't believe David would've bothered to see us perform even once. If he had come 'many' times I must really be blind because I hadn't seen him in the audience even once. The places we played weren't that big and generally I saw the people I knew when they came by. I supposed it was possible he'd lurked in shadows against the back walls. He said he particularly liked a song we did called "my love is a dove" and he sang a bit of the chorus. I was surprised because we hadn't done that one that day, and couldn't help but smile at the sound of his singing. His head swung about a bit as he finished the chorus and his hair tousled. He was being charming and I felt myself succumbing to his spell; so I looked up from the water ring my defrosting mug was making on the table and asked after Antra. He grimaced as he said they'd broken up a long time ago. That was the extent of what he said on that subject. I was unsure what 'a long time' meant to him. He added that he wasn't seeing anyone. I doubted whether that might be true.

The conversation moved to what groups influenced what the JIMJAMS played. This was familiar territory between us. David and I had initially bonded over shared musical and other cultural tastes. I figured he was trying to soften me up but I wasn't sure what for and in any case I got caught up in it. I couldn't help myself. Talking to him was just as enchanting as it had always been. Then David wanted to know about the guys and what we got up to. I ignored that question and asked him to fill me in on what he'd been up to. He spoke vaguely about different plays he'd been in and auditions for commercials. I thought it was strange he didn't go into every detail about his roles and reviews. I didn't imagine for a second he might've become humble. He'd spent a summer at Disney and hated it but had very funny stories about the escapades of all the actors and entertainers. He was captivating as he told me about his exploits under the sun surrounded by cartoon landscapes and happy holidaymakers. When I imagined him in his Tigger suit I laughed out loud and that made me realise I had been wound exceedingly tight up to that moment. Even so, it was frankly difficult for me to tear myself away from him. Talking to him felt like being home after a long exile, but I refused to give in to the longing to relax entirely with David. When my beer was finished I told him it was time for me to go. He looked dissatisfied with this, but he got up and went to the bar with me. David watched me say goodnight to everyone and leave.

During that week I am ashamed to say I could not take my mind off our encounter. I dreamt about David every night and woke up thinking of him. We'd spoken for about an hour but everything he'd said was etched in my memory. At any moment during the day I closed my eyes there was the vision of him. I could recall exactly what he'd worn, the crinkle around his eyes as he told his stories, the way he waved his hands around, how he lifted his beer mug to his mouth and his soft lips kissing the edge of the glass. I wondered how he'd learned the words to our song. Was it possible he actually had seen us perform more than that once? I didn't speak to anyone else about it though. I kept all of my emotional havoc and confusion to myself rather than have to open the hornets' nest of why a person who they never knew was more than a friend would have such a discombobulating effect on me.

The next weekend the JIMJAMS performed David was there again. None of my other friends had stopped by. He'd come on his own. This time I did spot him at the bar, looking nonchalant and handsome, before we started our first set. He didn't see me observe him as he was ordering at the bar and talking to another male I didn't know. His presence made me anxious like it was the first time we were performing. This annoyed me to no end given I actually hadn't been nervous at all the first time we'd done a gig in public. It was David's effect on me; making me insecure of my delivery. I hadn't ever considered caring what anyone else thought aside from the guys in the band, but I absolutely cared about David's opinion of anything at all he saw of me. Gladly, I did not forget the words or miss my cues. The set was at least as good as any other set we'd done that semester but I didn't feel the release or the confidence performing normally gave me. In our break I hid in the bathroom to avoid the possibility of having to speak to anyone let alone be observed by David in my insecure state. I redid my makeup several times; and then just stood there staring in the mirror while I contemplated what could David be after? What could he possibly want? It certainly wasn't me as he'd wrecked that. He didn't show remorse. He acted like nothing had happened. But despite everything I knew I felt the same for him. I was still angry about how he'd damaged me and hurt me, but I was also still in love and inconsolably confused.

After the second set David came straight up to the stage before we'd even put our stuff in the van and offered to buy us all a round. The guys were happy to accept free beer and it didn't matter to them who was buying. The five of us ended up sitting around a table and David got the guys to tell stories about themselves, how they'd met, how they'd gotten into their music… Then he started asking them to talk about me. From the questions he asked them and the way he directed the conversation; he seemed to be trying in a very roundabout way to learn what I did with all my time and whether I was dating anyone. He couldn't really care about that though, could he? Inside I laughed because the guys wouldn't know that much about anything that didn't happen in front of them. Even after so long my relationship with the guys in the band was primarily about the band. Truth was we only spent time together for band related things. Still, they did tell several stories about failed suitors; which was what David seemed to be after and which seemed to inspire great mirth in him. This time we had three rounds before we wrapped up and went our separate ways.

Again, I found myself thinking of naught but David throughout the week. When I ate with Randy and Dom they said he'd been singing one of the band's songs through the halls of their dorm; maddening the shit out of everyone who was trying to study. I was elated they had brought this up because I could never have done it. I asked; in as offhand a manner I could muster, if had he joined them to see us play other times? Actually he had; they said. He'd been tagging along ever since he and Antra broke up; but never stayed too long and always left early to go do theatre stuff. How had I never noticed him? Did I spend too much time singing with my eyes closed? Was David actually enshrouded by impenetrable dark matter? Had I only observed him the last time standing at the bar because he'd wanted me to? I wondered at this just as Dom went into a rant about what a flibbertigibbet David was.

Dom couldn't stand how girls kept tripping all over themselves for such a shallow prick. I asked then why did they hang out with him? Randy said "oh, he's not that bad. He's good for a laugh. Besides, he's not getting us into bed is he?" I smiled as the conversation turned to Randy and Dom's comparative degrees of masculinity and heterosexuality, but I hadn't realised they both thought David was trivial. I never thought David was an Einstein but he was so fascinating to me I never stopped to gauge what sort of impression he made on other people. We had all hung out together so assiduously in the first year I hadn't realised Randy and Dom felt he was marginal to their group. I should have taken more stock of what my oldest friends thought. As it happened I only managed to absorb that David definitely wasn't seeing Antra anymore and that he knew our songs well enough to sing them in front of others. That couldn't possibly be a show for me could it? The chances he'd calculated doing that so that Randy would mention it to me were nil.

The remainder of the week my thoughts seemed to be on a Ferris wheel, repeating the same themes and ideas in a repetitive cycle. I would think about what David had done to me in our freshman year, then feel the love and the deception simultaneously, then think about his face during our recent encounters, and what Dom and Randy had said. I was still completely obsessed. No interaction with anyone through the week was able to break into my meditation on David for more than a minute or so. Worse yet, when I got ready for the next gig I realised I was getting dressed for him. I was rechecking myself in the mirror an inordinate number of times and re-doing my eyes in a way I hadn't done them for over a year. When he didn't show up that Friday I was more than disappointed. True, we were playing off campus in a townie bar that wasn't that well known, but it was an empty evening that made me feel alone in a way I hadn't felt since my horrible summer of disillusionment. Mostly I was angry with myself for having wanted to see him at all. How could I have thought he'd seriously want to see me for me, rather than as a passing fancy because there was nothing better to do? I went directly home when we'd put our kit away and scolded myself for having keenly anticipated talking to him.

The following week I tried to push him from my mind. I told myself I wasn't allowed to ponder him. I wouldn't let myself do it knowingly but I ended up subconsciously drifting to David every time there was a lull in my thoughts. It was like being on a diet and continuously going back to the fridge to see the only thing in it was a forbidden chocolate cake. I'd shut the door and walk away resolute to stick to my diet; only to return a short while later with unsatisfied hunger to stare at the cake and tell myself I wasn't allowed to have it. I made it through the week and convinced myself I would never see him again as I got dressed for the next gig. And when we unloaded the van to my genuine surprise there was David sitting at a table with a couple of guys I didn't know. He waved and Angel and Harry waved back before I did. They said they'd run into him on campus mid-week and they thought he was a pretty decent dude. I frowned because it felt suspect to me; but I knew deep down I was probably just jealous they'd been in contact with him while I had been struggling to force him from my mind.

After we played Angel and Harry led the way to sit at David's table. The guys that had been with him had left. We had drinks and more drinks, then more, and then the guys left but I stayed behind. I am not sure if it was the alcohol, the amount of time we'd been sitting together, the release after a week of trying to proscribe David from my consciousness, or simply the smell of him so close and the look of his jawbone. I was powerless in his thrall despite telling myself over and over 'you cannot trust him' 'don't believe a word he says' 'he's hiding something'. I just missed him so much and missed feeling the kind of connection we had far too much to continue resisting. When we were alone at the table he put his right hand against my temple and pushed his fingers into my hair. His touch was electric and I was tachycardic with the thrill of it. Looking me in the eyes with absolute sincerity he said "Cherie, I've missed you so much. I can't stand it." My will melted right there and when I breathed out I realised my body had been rigid from the degree of distrust I felt. That was all gone now as David recovered his dominion. I knew I was being reckless but I wanted some respite from the constant internal struggle against my own feelings. I didn't say anything I just leaned toward him and he met me halfway to kiss me.

We went to my apartment (I didn't live in the dorms anymore) and I felt the anticipation on the way there just as much as I had any other time he'd followed me to my bed. David balked at my making him use a condom but he did put it on when I told him without it he might as well go home. I might be passionately foolish but I had certainly learned better than to trust him on that score. Once past that we were ardent and I was delirious. I was an addict having a fix after a long dry spell. It was the first time I'd truly felt happy since I'd sat in Glenda Cooper's office. It was a fantastic moment. I didn't think about anything other than what he was doing to me and with me right there and then. I was so caught up in the joy of having him back, feeling him, tasting him; that as we orgasmed I verbalized "I love you David." I hadn't been able to help myself. I was overwhelmed after having fought so hard to control my feelings for so long. David stopped moving and while he was still inside me he looked at my face like he was surprised to see me underneath him. His expression turned to apprehension. He sat back slapping his forehead with one hand as he said "What am I doing here? I need to go back to Antra." Now I was confused. I asked him "Did I do something wrong? What did I do wrong?" He just said "I just shouldn't be here. This was a mistake. You don't understand. Antra really gets me." He might as well have pulverized my brains by clubbing me over the head. I was stunned and dumbfounded. In the time it took me to clear my head to appreciate what he was saying he was dressed and had gone out the door. He hadn't said anything else to me or cared how I might feel. He hadn't even said goodbye.

It was my own fault. I knew it was my own fault. I had let my loneliness get the better of me and despite knowing better I had let David back into my head. I had let my love for him override my intelligence and the certainty that he would do me harm. At least this time I'd made him wear a condom. I sat staring at the ceiling with my brain on pause. Eventually I realised there were tears streaming down the sides of my face because the pillow was getting wet and the damp cloth was uncomfortable. I felt a broken shell. No, in fact I was just a void. I was nothing if he treated me like nothing. He'd demonstrated AGAIN that to him I was just a hole for him to use when a better one wasn't available. Earlier that night I had felt like I'd come back home. Now I was bare on the street with no possessions and no harbour on the horizon.

It was incomprehensible to me that I should care so deeply for a person who obviously didn't care about me at all. If I felt so strongly how was it possible he felt nothing? Was his makeup somehow fundamentally different? Was it me? Was I actually abnormal? I pondered whether my feelings of love were comparable to a mental disorder. If some clinical affective disease existed then there might be a treatment or cure. Perhaps my genetic structure made me predisposed to feel love differently than others. Really though, the only thing that mattered to me was that I was not what he wanted. My body seemed to be shutting down as despair took over. I couldn't move. I felt nauseous and my head was aching; apparently from the silent crying. I couldn't even wipe the tears from my face. I couldn't be bothered to turn the pillow over. I was tired of staring at the ceiling so I closed my eyes but kept on cursing my lack of sense until I eventually passed out from exhaustion.

The next morning I was still naked in bed when Dom called on the phone; waking me up. I was supposed to have met him for brunch. I had completely forgotten. I wasn't smart enough to cancel on him. I thought if I did that I'd have to create an excuse and I'd surely –sooner or later– fail at maintaining the fiction. We'd known each other so long it was exceedingly difficult to lie to or hide things from Dom without him realising. I apologised and said I'd make it up to him if he came over; giving me time to shower and dress. I didn't think about what I might look like because it was just Dom. I threw something clean on without much thought to what it was. I made a full hot breakfast and Bloody Marys for him. It was difficult because I kept breaking into sobs and having to choke them down to avoid letting the food burn. I did manage to do it; but it seemed an extraordinary effort and I ended up wishing I'd just cancelled or said I was ill. Enduring the entire morning hiding how I felt was going to be problematic and awkward. I suppressed everything I was feeling and decided I wouldn't think about anything at all until Dom was gone. I'd blank my mind. I couldn't tell Dom what I'd done. I couldn't tell him what a moron I was. I couldn't tell him I was dying inside when he showed up at the door.

Dom arrived just as I was finishing the cooking and I put on a brave face for him. He was no fool though. He knew me well enough to know something was wrong. I could only avoid the abyss by focusing on specifically what he said and I wasn't really speaking much which; truly, was not like me. My stomach was churning with self-loathing and sorrow and I had zero appetite. I made an effort to drink while he ate. Swallowing made me aware of how dry my throat was. Maybe I was dehydrated from all the crying? We sat next to each other on a two-seater sofa watching music videos on a 16" black and white tv I'd picked up at a yard sale. It minimised the need to speak to him but he saw I wasn't eating. He stared at me for a bit before saying I should just tell him what was on my mind. Weren't we good enough friends for me to share with him? I said it was nothing I was just out of sorts. He asked how much vodka had I put in the drinks? I wasn't actually sure. I said twice what the recipe called for because I was having a shitty morning until he'd come by. I wanted to burst into sobs as this brief mention of my mood (and the thought of the cause of it) made me realise I did want to talk to someone. I bit my tongue but now I was afraid of how far down the self-pity hole I might fall when he left. At least having him there made me stifle it for a while. I thought I'd have the rest of the day and all night every night to relive my humiliation and hurt in detail.

When we'd finished eating we made a new batch of Bloody Marys even though Dom complained it was going to his head. I asked him what else did he have to do? Nothing. We picked up the plates and stood next to each other washing up. Then out of nowhere; while I was turned toward him putting a plate on the drainer, he put his arms around me and kissed me on the mouth. I think maybe I was moist eyed and he felt sorry for me? I was surprised to say the least that he kissed me. I'd never thought of him in a sexual way. He was my friend not a potential love interest. I didn't stop him though. I was feeling so low and empty his touch was a comforting reprieve from my self-contempt. He put his hand on my breast and I realised in my rush to get dressed I had forgotten to put a bra on. Had he thought I was coming on to him? Maybe he'd misinterpreted my relative silence and awkwardness as something else?

I wasn't turned on but I felt consoled and I let him have his way. It's an archaic expression I know, but I wasn't into him that way and I wasn't in any frame of mind to give into anything primal. He didn't say anything either. He kept kissing me and he held me close, then he stepped back to take his shirt off and unbelt his trousers. What was I thinking while this happened? Dom's manner of kissing was strange. He stuck his tongue into my mouth but didn't move his lips much; didn't really connect with my own mouth. David's kissing was very active constant lip lock with back of the mouth all over the teeth movement; and to me that was second nature. I also observed in a detached way that Dom had gained a lot of weight since coming to college. He was a swimmer in high school so I'd seen him practically naked quite a few times; just not fully so. I also felt less calm when he stepped back; not that I was very calm to begin with. Despite not really wanting him, Dom's holding me had made me feel desirable; which after David's rejection the night before was more than welcome. I suppose I was truthfully on autopilot because my rational mind was busy fighting to expel David from my thoughts; but Dom didn't force me into anything. I shut off my brain and my feelings as best I could and concentrated on the motions.

I didn't take my own clothes off. When Dom was naked; except for his socks, he started kissing me again and he moved me to the couch. I was wearing a pullover dress and he pushed the bottom up and pulled my underwear off. I guess because I didn't feel attracted to him or aroused by him -because he was just a friend- and I was focusing on the specific minutia of his actions to avoid the David chasm; I started analysing how he was doing what he was doing. This was rogue territory between us but his touch was brutish and he was fumbling. It couldn't have been inexperienced. He'd had a few girls over the years I'd known him. Perhaps he'd never really concerned himself with whether they were satisfied? I wasn't sure. I'd always thought Dom was a sensitive guy. As I was ruminating this he was leaned over me thrusting and I was amazed that having him inside me I still felt nothing but indifference to what he was doing, or maybe curiosity about how different it was from what I was used to.

Well, that's not entirely true. I wondered what Dom feeling was? I wondered what had made him decide to make a move after years of us both keeping the friend zone crystal clear. I watched his face. He had his eyes closed but his brow was furrowed like he was making a huge effort. I wondered how long was he going to take to finish? He seemed to be taking forever… I started feeling exasperated. What had I done? What was he going to expect from me now? What the hell was I doing? Then he started groaning and he pulled out and his ejaculate sprayed all over my torso, and even on my dress that was scrunched up around my neck. Jesus Christ! I was so out of it I hadn't asked him to put a condom on. Violent repulsion snapped me out of my remoteness from what was happening. What the hell was he thinking? I scooted back and sat up; wiping his semen off of me with the hem of my dress as I pulled it down my body to cover myself. "What the fuck was that Dom?" He said "I don't want to get you pregnant Cherie." I can't explain why I was enraged by those words; but I felt like I'd just been used in place of a blow-up doll.

Where the hell did he get off saying he didn't want to get me pregnant? I yelled "First of all, that is not contraception. If you want contraception, I'm on the pill; but you should've used a condom if you want to be sure of that." He was puzzled. "Cherie, what's the big deal?" "The big deal is you've just sprayed all over me like I'm not even here. What the fuck are you having sex with me for?" Dom looked irked as he said "Whoa, really?" I didn't miss a beat "Really Dom. Why the hell are you treating me like a prostitute?" His jaw dropped. He said "What are you talking about?" I couldn't explain it. I didn't know myself. I only knew I was angry enough to throttle him. I wanted to punch him in the face. Was he god's gift to women? I told him to get the fuck out of my apartment. As he was getting dressed he said "Cherie, I'm sorry. This was a mistake." That made me livid. He was the second man to say that to me in less than a day. From a rumbling visceral place I shouted "Just leave. Leave me alone."

Dom left and we didn't genuinely speak anymore after that. Our friendship died that day. I didn't have to say anything to anyone because he withdrew. When we ran into each other we were cordial but he never spent more than two minutes in a ten-meter radius of me. To be honest, every time I saw him I felt the urge to punch him or slap him and I'm sure the hostility was evident. Randy thought it was strange at first but didn't pry. The anger only lasted while I was looking at Dom though. When Dom was out of sight I fell right back into my deep-rooted multifaceted distress over David.

A couple of weeks after the second worst 24 hour period of my life (the absolute worst having been discovery of miscarriage on the heels of discovery of STD's); Randy said Dom had told him that Dom and I had had sex and it was a mistake. This was at a lunch a deux. Randy didn't need any more information than to know we'd slept together to just leave it be. He didn't take sides but Randy thought Dom had had a thing for me; which I knew could not be true. Dom had never once done anything whatsoever to make me think he was in the least interested and we'd known each other for years and years. The same day Randy told me he'd spoken with Dom about us; he told me he'd met up with David. Randy specifically wanted me to know David and Becky had done a TV commercial for a local van dealership. He was very particular about it. Apparently, the TV commercial was inspired by my band. I didn't watch a lot of TV; aside from music videos and cartoons, so I hadn't seen it. Randy told me what programs to watch so I might have a chance. Of course, nothing else could enter my mind from the moment he told me until I'd seen it. I skipped classes to stay home and waited through various shows I had no interest in for David's commercial to come on.

When I finally did see the commercial; my emotions crossed an event horizon. David played Angel, Becky played me, Harry was played by a guy in a gorilla suit, and Hugo was a Shaggy (from Scooby Doo) caricature. Becky's portrayal of me included a very accurate direct copy of one of my favourite outfits, and she had done her makeup exactly the same as mine right down to the colour palette. The band in their commercial seemed to be either high or intellectually disabled. They were like the 2001 monkeys trying to figure out how to get their gear in the van. Each time they tried; when things didn't fit, Becky's version of me kept saying "Did I do something wrong? What did I do wrong?". Their dilemma was finally solved by buying a new van. It was supposed to be rip roaring hilarious I'm sure. When Becky said "Did I do something wrong? What did I do wrong?" my heart went hypernova. Every time she repeated it; which was a few times during the single commercial but innumerable by the end of a day of possessed TV watching to catch it again and again and again, every time my heart got smaller and darker and more compressed. Had he told her what he'd done with me that night? Had they laughed about me together? Had they analysed together the inflection of my voice so she could mimic it? Did I need any more objective evidence that David didn't give a flying fuck about me? I tried to scrutinise his facial expressions to see if it revealed anything about what was going on behind his eyes. There was no clue there.

I was so lost and dejected and had been dying inside for so many days already; when I finished watching the commercial (because the channel didn't broadcast after 3 am) I literally wanted to end it all. I had been crying and sobbing for hours with my bewildered mind in a recursive loop of pain that was ever magnifying. I still couldn't speak to anyone I knew about it though; without making things a lot worse. I was desperate for someone to talk to so I called the suicide hotline. Speaking to the person on the other end of the line was more than frustrating because they wouldn't listen to me or my problems; they simply kept insisting I must go for a psych evaluation the next morning. They weren't there to talk to me they said, only to take note and pass my case on. Finally I wrote the time and place down and hung up. I fell asleep crying on the sofa with the TV bleep in the background, and woke up due to the sound of the morning news report.

When I went to the appointment the next day the psychiatrist remarked I was overly made up and said this was a sign of depression. People either let themselves go or put too much into their appearance. I had been doing this for over a year. Had I been depressed for over a year? In an hour I only managed to give him highlights of what had happened; but by the end of it he had diagnosed me as cyclothymic and prescribed me Prozac. I spent the remainder of my college experience in psychiatric therapy and on drugs (prescribed ones but drugs all the same); all from the campus doctors and all hidden from my parents.

Being on Prozac curbed my drinking habit as you're not supposed to mix serotonin inhibitors with alcohol; and I suppose that got me into better shape. Over a great many sessions the psychiatrist determined that my suffering was not exaggerated as the events that had happened to me indeed deserved appropriate serious processing. I felt on the one hand vindicated that what had happened to me was NOT ok and not normal. It was David who had done wrong and my reaction to it was understandable. On the other hand; it seemed to confirm I did not have any affective disorder so my broken heart was just a broken heart. That was hard to swallow. I questioned whether that part of the assessment was right. I still have never met anyone else so debilitated by love. Maybe the rest of the world is just a lot better at putting on a brave face; or faking. But if you're faking in everyday life then what's the point? Even though this man said my reactions were understandable I still felt like a Tennessee Williams lead. The psychiatrist clarified: my reactions were understandable but I was still cyclothymic.

Meantime I had decided I was much happier on the drugs so I pushed back whenever the psychiatrist suggested reducing or withdrawing them. I exaggerated or highlighted the right kind of behaviour to remind him of my obsessive nature. I told him I panicked when my dosage was reduced. Finally I told him my atheism made me feel lost and alone. That was pure bullshit, but he found it difficult to imagine not believing in a god so I worked with that. Let's face it, we are all genuinely alone in this world and being cognizant of the fact is just facing reality. No two people share the same life experience or interpretation of events; not wholly. Also, I don't need a god to help me sleep at night. I need to be ok with my reality. If my reality is unacceptable hoping there is another one to go to when I die won't resolve my issues here and now. Only I can fix it by changing something about my reality. If it is beyond my control then I'm stuffed but that's life. Believing a myth to make myself feel better about or deny my insignificance to the world, universe or history just seems mindless to me.

Being on Prozac was great. I functioned like clockwork and never cared too much about anything at all while I was on it. It didn't change what I thought about anything; Prozac just took the sting off by liberating me from having to have feelings about any of it. People could insult me to my face and I didn't react. People asked me to do things I didn't want to and I didn't mind so much. I was malleable and congenial. I could be with people or alone; I wasn't bothered. It made performing with the JIMJAMS easier because I focused only on my delivery; but it also quelled any creativity so I no longer wrote poetry or lyrics. It was like letting my autonomous functions rule but retaining just enough of my intellect to do what I was supposed to do and get through classes. It made holidays at home infinitely more bearable.

When college was finished I had to come off the Prozac as private insurance wouldn't cover it; but more so because I didn't want any history of psychiatric treatment to be on any record that any employer might see. The adjustment back to experiencing emotions was difficult;

but thankfully not cold turkey. It was progressive. It was like letting the blood flow back into limbs that have fallen asleep; with pricking tingling discomfort. Being aware of the return to sensation helped me to analyse all of my reactions, gauge them, measure them, and tie them down when they weren't appropriate.

So I moved on with chemical assistance, and when that was taken away it had been about 18 months from the 24 hours of shame, and also that long since I'd had any notable exchange with either David or Dom. It's funny how people; who are crucial to your everyday and your understanding of your own identity, can crudely drop out of existence. Whether you like it or not the globe continues turning, seasons follow seasons, you get older and, unless you end it by your own hand or you die some other way; you endure despite yourself.

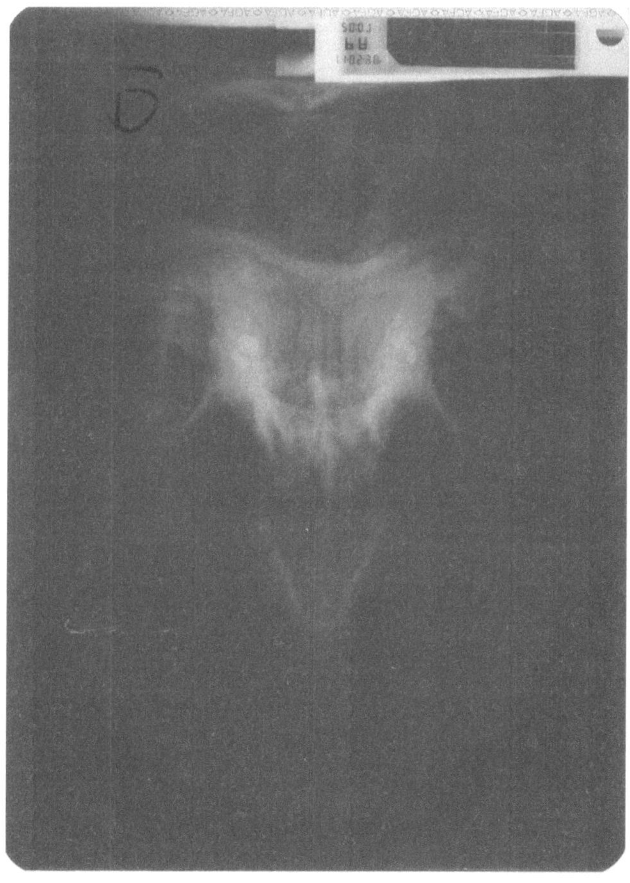

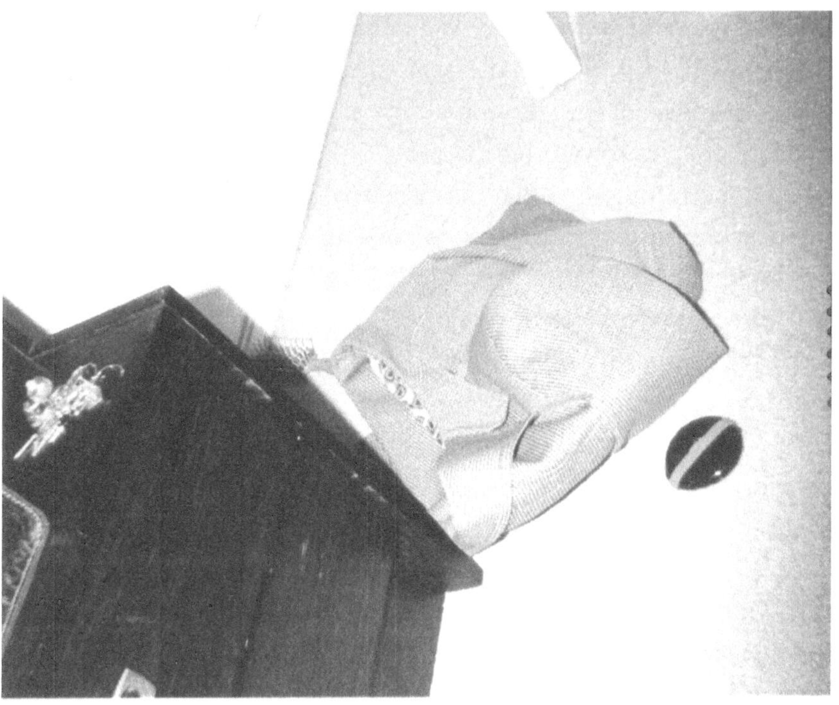

My last significant accident (fingers crossed – I'm not dead yet) was a week after I moved to Scotland. Thus, once again, my life was jumbled midway through June. I had moved up there with my entire household in tow. Seeking to escape a life of dismal prospects, I had spent everything down to my last cent on relocating my life to start over. My job was going to be easy and I would live a relaxed life in the country. This was rural Scotland. Deer and owls are not uncommon. Bunnies abound on the greens. The roads get blocked in winter from snow and in summer from floods. The towns are far apart and no one could live day to day without a car, unless they were independently wealthy and had everything delivered.

Moving across countries with the entirety of my worldly possessions was expensive. I planned to spend the rest of my life in this new place and had left nothing behind. Of course, this means including my cat. I don't understand people who leave pets behind just because they move, or for any reason really. A pet is a commitment you take on and not to be entered into lightly. Anyway, I had just moved into a cute little house with a small garden with all my stuff and it took me a week to unpack and put everything in its right place. Unfortunately, moving into a house on my own had not been part of my plan. My employer went back on his word to provide me accommodation when he saw I had brought a cat along. This despite the business being pet-friendly and him taking his pet to work with him every day and me having explained before coming that I was bringing one.

So given the job was a minimum wage one; my final cost of living was more than I'd calculated. I couldn't afford to turn the heat on. The electricity was on a card meter that kept running out every 24 hours no matter how much cash I put on it. I needed groceries and this meant I needed more cash. On the first available afternoon I aimed to take some stuff to town to sell. After work I set out in the sheeting rain in my European left hand wheel car on the unfamiliar rural Scottish road. Driving between fields of strawberries I was only going 40mph in a 50 zone; around a bend, when the car skidded on mud and started to spin like a horizontal pinwheel. It slammed into the side of an overpass crushing what would have been the driver side if I'd been in a local car. The skidding must have added momentum because smashing into the concrete made the car bounce back and green vegetation came off the underpass and covered my windshield. I had my seatbelt on *of course*, so even though the car was written off I got out of it mentally shaken but physically ok. A neighbour who'd seen me move in saw me standing next to the smashed car and stopped. He remarked that if I'd been in a car with the wheel on the right I might be dead, judging by the condition of the car. He waited with me until the police came by. I was so lucky I had bothered to make sure I had roadside assistance on my insurance; that gave me a cover car. I would've lost my job without it, but by the end of that same day I had a replacement car to park in front of my newly rented house. I had to wait until the next day to eat because I hadn't made it in time to sell anything in town.

At work the next Monday my boss; an out of shape man, rushed in breathing heavy from jogging. When I looked up to say hi his face was perplexed and visibly relieved at the same time. When he didn't see my car in the car park he'd thought I'd not come back. I gave highlights of what had happened and said that my car had to be written off (was totalled so to speak). He didn't ask or care about the accident or how it might affect me; just that I was still coming in to cover the rota. I overheard the same man say to one of the customers another time that you couldn't get to involved with the staff because they would drag you down into their mess.

Of course the Scots have a special sensibility. A few months after my own accident a motorcyclist was killed when he tried to cross a one-lane bridge against the light and was hit by an oncoming truck. Apparently he burned to death when his gas tank exploded and his clothes caught on fire because no one taught him to stop drop and roll. Literally the morning after; just a few hours from it having happened, when I went in to work the staff were all trying to one up each other with their jokes about the human torch.

Back to me: As my car had been totalled and written off I had to get a new one. This was not covered by my third party only insurance. I had to max out my credit to get a cheap third hand car, and this meant I would be in debt for the next three years as making minimum wage I could never manage to pay off the principal. I really didn't splash out on the car. I was just truly broke when it happened and subsequently THAT poor. Every month the interest grew and in attempts to get ahead of the arrears I took on a second and then a third job. I ended up working approximately ninety hours a week for about two of the three years it took me to pay off the cost of the car. I gained forty pounds because I could only afford to eat bargains from the store and the cheapest food was always stale baked goods. It was a special day when I made it in time to get items discounted because they would expire, before they were bought up by someone else. Combine the nearly all carbs diet with nearly ninety hours a week of different sedentary roles and I had no way to avoid the weight gain. My rapidly increasing size and just as rapidly declining health proved to me that no one cares about anyone else at work. Not a single person in any of my three workplaces ever expressed concern, or cared to know if anything might be wrong, or wondered why I never had a single hour of free time for three long horrible years. If I saw someone gain forty pounds in months I think I would at least wonder if they were ok. I suppose they assumed my dietary habits were just poor and I was simply antisocial. How would they know if they were only work colleagues and the underlying belief was that one should not mix with the staff? Don't ask don't tell… I'm sure they made a slew of unjustified assumptions on my motivations and character because they never took the time to know who I was or my background.

So my great starting over in life was quashed about a week after I relocated it. I never had a chance to do any of the things I had aimed to do because I never got ahead of the debt. Finally after three years I managed to pay if off but this was not because my hard work got me recognition or a raise, not because I had counted every single penny every single day and thought of nothing but how I would afford to pay my bills, not because I went three years without watching television or going to the movies or eating out or having any holiday. I managed to pay it off because I ended up having a stroke and in hospital I was strong armed into contacting my parents and asking them to settle my debt. Which I did and they did. I might as well have called them up to ask them to slit my throat as that was the day I said goodbye to ever being able to live any life resembling anything like what I had wanted.

By the way, the dealer that sold me my beater told me the spot on the road where I'd skidded and hit the underpass had had very many accidents over the years. People didn't realise that in farm lands the roads are dirty and when it rains it turns to mud and there is zero traction in mud. Twice he'd seen people lose their legs there. I was lucky (he thought) I had only been going 40mph. I asked him why didn't they put some kind of sign to warn of the sharp turn? The reply was that would cost the town money…

⤝∞⤞

My belief in love or the idea that anyone might ever want me in anything approaching an amorous way was completely destroyed. Decimated. Lay waste until there was naught but dust that blew away in the winds of the cosmos never to cohere into any substance again. Whenever I thought about it I knew there must be something wrong with me because no one around me suffered this way. As years went by my friends had relationships, got married, had kids that they liked and watched grow up. A few got divorced but they moved on or started over. Other friends dated and dated and flowed in and out of people's lives with ease. But I never trusted anyone enough to let my guard down ever again.

Well, that's not true entirely. Eventually it wasn't a matter of trust it was simply lack of interest because repetition of failure was tedious and I frankly didn't like wasting my time with people I had no connection with when I might be doing something that was more engaging. People seemed to think it was fear; which in my opinion wasn't true. What I saw in a lot of those people was conformity with what was close by and familiar rather than a relationship founded in love between equals or love of any genuinely meaningful depth. It seemed to me a lot of them had done what was necessary to keep the bed warm with someone that wasn't too difficult to get along with regardless of what their real feelings were. Categorically I thought they were the cowards. How afraid of being alone do you have to be to put up with shit from a person you no longer even like (if you ever did truly) and not contemplate splitting from them? Not all of them were economically trapped. It was pretty clear where these people's real feelings lay when you heard them talk about their own respective REAL "him" or "her" despite not having seen "him" or "her" for many years. Suddenly they would animate and show feelings they had buried or forgotten, and it would be clear that their day to day partner was a poor substitute. I had no interest in pretending I had feelings I did not have just to avoid being alone. It wasn't about not wanting to put up with someone who doesn't put the toothpaste cap back on right; it was about not wanting to feel like a prostitute just to be able to split expenses. I would have liked to have kids, but not just anyone's. People go to sperm banks when they are desperate for motherhood and good on them. I didn't feel that way. I couldn't have done it on my own and I didn't want to tie myself for the rest of my life to a man I didn't feel everything for just to get his sperm.

As an example: my friend Dom, with whom I reconciled years after because he sent me a friend request on Facebook; had ended up being one of those people who entangled himself in a soul crushing relationship. He spent a decade alienating every woman who tried to love him because either they or their desire to have offspring didn't fit into his personal professional development plan. When he hit 30 it was on his schedule to have kids but none of the women he'd wanted to have them with "one day" were around any longer. He told me none of his family had ever married for love, so he didn't see it as a bad thing when he chose to enter an arrangement with a friend that was afraid of time running out on her biological clock. They both wanted kids and they were both without anyone else to have them with; so they decided to just do it. He shared their wedding pictures with me. It had been a handful of people at the justice of the peace. I'd seen happier faces on people at funerals and I told him so. He said sure; it was just one of the agreed steps in their arrangement but really there was nothing to celebrate that day. His wife had been pissed off the judge wouldn't shut up about love because she had never hidden she was settling as she'd not found love. He didn't feel it either but had thought feelings would grow with time.

Their first five years were super overloaded busy with raising the baby and there was no space for anything but the baby. But then the baby started going to school and talking, and he started to have time to think for himself and breathe on his own. The baby started commenting how other people's mommy's and daddy's looked at each other in a way he never saw Dom look at mommy. Dom told me his day to day home life had become a cumulus of business transactions that were relentlessly summed in his wife's ledger. The friendship they'd started with had dissipated and nothing but obligations and tit for tat took its place. Everything in the household was subject to contract-like terms except for how he felt for his kid. Was it worth it to have done it to have his kid? He certainly wanted and loved his son but he realised he'd made a stupid and unnecessary sacrifice by getting married to a person he never thought about with anything approaching passion. He was wistful about a couple of women he'd rather have spent his days with if only they would have waited for him.

After five years and a baby he didn't feel more for the mother of his child than he did for co-workers he'd seen every day for a decade. The worst part in his mind was that he suspected she was actually a lesbian because they hadn't had sex more than a dozen times in five years. He might as well have just signed a shared custody contract and donated sperm for all the home life he enjoyed and shared companionship he got. He thought it might've been better to have hired a surrogate. He didn't need me to tell him he'd made a mistake that doesn't need to be made in the 21st-century western world. He finally got divorced with shared custody, and was much happier not having to mete out his personal space with a person who only cared about what he did for her rather than himself or his happiness or what might cross his mind. I couldn't conceive of entering into a strained arrangement like what he'd had, but then people often tell me I don't understand convention. For me being with a person out of obligation or habit or settling just isn't good enough.

I tried to make myself go out with people on occasion just to get friends to leave me alone about the fact that I never did. It didn't work because I could never disguise well enough that I wasn't in the least interested. Usually to save time I'd just tell the guy before the end of dinner I couldn't see us having a second date unless it were in a purely platonic way, and we'd split the cheque because they weren't interested in friendship. My friends tried to get me to use dating services and I refused. When mobile apps came on the scene they installed Tinder on my phone in a last-ditch attempt against my will. I remember scrolling through about 100 pictures with them at different points in time. Every single one repulsed me. It was a collection of bald fat football fans; most of which had been divorced or had small children, or who didn't see anything wrong with posting pictures of themselves unshaven and wearing rumpled exercise clothes in situations when they weren't exercising (or on bodies that had apparently never been inside anything approaching a gym). A lot of them posted photos with their previous girlfriend or wife, when they didn't just post a torso without a face. And there were sooo many with no photo, that my friends confirmed meant they were cheating. To me it was repugnant and no paragraph summary of interests could make up for the clear overriding message they really just wanted to get laid and either didn't believe in paying for it or somehow thought they were coming off as something other than sexually aggressive bastards. Finally there was a report on the news that stated that in just one year approximately 2000 women in the city had been raped by men they met using the app. My friends left me alone about it after that.

I never found another person that shared more than one or two interests and attitudes or that I was genuinely attracted to. No one else ever entered my brain through my eyes. No one else was ever worth any effort on my part. I never found anyone else again that I was happy to talk to about anything or everything under the sun and who was also interested in hearing what I might say (or at least feigning it convincingly given I did realise David hadn't been genuine with me). In truth, I hadn't gone after David either since he'd pinned me against a tree, followed me and kept coming back to me, so I suppose I never had any romantic initiative to begin with. Also; despite everything and not wanting to, I never stopped feeling devotion to him. In spite of the humiliation, the rejection and cruelty, the disease, the dead foetus (that I could never bring myself to think about for too long as it was so painful to consider - I invariably shut off completely); I was absolutely and unconditionally addicted.

So to help myself I stopped talking to people David and I knew in common unless they were out of touch with him. That effectively meant I no longer spoke to anyone from college since all the guys from the dorm were his friend first and the girls I knew disappeared from the face of the earth as they moved and changed their names on getting married.

I avoided every place I ever thought I might run into him. The way I felt was a pervasive problem that cut across every aspect of my life. Nothing would fix it or get rid of it so I just shut it in a box and stored it away under the bed. I mean there's no kind of anonymous therapy group for idiots who love people that don't care about them is there? I wasn't a victim of wife abuse (assuming a non-spouse might be allowed to categorise oneself in that sort of grouping); just a moron who couldn't stop loving a complete jerk no matter what he came up with next.

According to Juanes one late year is worth more than 100 years of solitude; but I guess it depends on who and how. Skip to fifteen years after David and I had finished. I had become a writer for a local paper in Atlanta and covered cultural events. My co-workers hated me because I was all about the job and never had any issues to stay late or cover holidays. This got me into a position where my boss counted on me and I got more interesting work than the others out of it. After about a year I learned they thought I was a lesbian but I never bothered to clear it up because it made life easier if I never had to deal with cheesy deceptive flirting.

By now David was starting to get work in films and was on a shoot in the city when I was asked to get some interviews out of the stars for a Sunday filler piece. There wasn't any wiggle room to get out of it because I'd never made excuses before. I thought if I so much as whispered a fuss my boss would refocus his favour on a younger and hungrier writer. I dreaded the upcoming reunion/interview but planned for it. After a couple of days I realised I'd abruptly started dieting without having actually decided I needed to lose weight. I was uncharacteristically taking the stairs instead of the elevator.

The thought of seeing David had woken up a part of me that had lain dormant for well over a decade, if not the full span of time since we'd finished. It was contemplation of what the opposite sex might perceive me to be and the prospect it would be less than I wanted it to be. I hadn't given a flying shit about anyone's opinion of my physique since I'd shut off my sexuality when I closed the chapter on David. Now, apparently, David was capable of getting it out of hibernation.

On my next day off I was at the cosmetics counter in a department store that I hadn't visited in a very long time either, and disheartened when the teenager behind it offered me an anti-wrinkle cream ideal for the middle aged. I asked her if it looked like I really needed it as I was still only 35. She gasped so I ended up buying one.

At the coffee machine at work the receptionist asked me if I had a new girlfriend because she'd never seen me smile like that before. My mind had wandered thinking about what it would be like to see him. I snorted and walked away.

Two weeks later, five pounds lighter and wearing trendy eye colours; I was standing in the lobby of what locally was considered the posh hotel although in downtown Chicago it would've been low end of the scale. Standing in the lobby I was checking my watch and looking in the mirror; before going to the reception desk to ask them to ring David's room. He was supposed to be in the bar but wasn't, and his agent and the press agent for the film were both AWOL as well. He wasn't well known enough yet to worry about being spotted but you never know. Maybe he had some die-hard fans from one of his TV sci-fi roles he might want to avoid. The teenager at the desk who rang his room for me giggled as she said "he's saying you should go on up he's waiting for you. It's room 1609." So up I went in the elevator checking again in the reflection that everything I had on was in the right place and my face wasn't too shiny. I looked middle aged and that was disappointing.

When I got out of the elevator he was standing there waiting. There he was in a casual suit and leather shoes; looking more in shape than the most recent pictures I'd seen of him in publicity releases. Time folded and I was 17 again being smiled at by him that first day in the dorms. Butterflies dispersed at high velocity in countless trajectories inside my gut. I was frozen as I observed his eyes had become a paler shade of blue with the years, and he had some grey in his hair. "Cherie! So happy to see you! How are you?" He stretched out his arms. It was so inviting I sensed a tug as my torso tried to go forward but my brain kept my feet put. I wasn't sure how I felt about this panorama so I started fussing with my shoulder bag; getting my notebook and avoiding eye contact while I considered it.

I thought about the strong connection to him I had felt throughout the years. I'd see photos of him where he'd chosen clothes that matched my own style. In interviews he spoke about music I listened to and books I'd read. Not top of the charts but obscure selections. His Hollywood causes were things I cared about. Despite the years of no communication deep inside I knew we were still on the same wavelength but not that he'd cared. Being convinced he didn't; years before I had taken the wild beast that was my unbridled feelings for him and gagged it and straight-jacketed it. Standing before him that beast was still locked in a cage in a basement in my mind but I could hear it trying to scream and thrashing about in its restraints. For over a decade having this locked down had meant I never had to think about what David had done to me or how I felt about it or how I felt about him. Not thinking about any of it at all was infinitely better than suffering every day with the awareness of being without him; of having to make a daily pledge like an alcoholic that I would not give in to feelings for him. But here he was standing in front of me and looking at me like nothing was wrong with me being in the same city as him. As if the continuum in my brain weren't imploding; I took a breath. I remembered he had come to the city I lived in so how this went was not all down to him.

I asked him if I'd missed an update about the meeting and he said he'd come up a day earlier than most of the people on the film. He'd asked his agent to arrange the interview with the paper because he wasn't sure if I'd go for it. When he found out he would be spending time in Atlanta he'd wanted to spend some time with me -one on one- before the work started. He was aware I might not be over the moon about it. Hmmm. He wanted to see *me* then? This was hard to believe since he was the one that disappeared after he started dating a string of girls I heard about via Randy; that all ended up more publicly unhappy than myself given my full relationship with him was not common knowledge. This of course before he'd started on his string of starlets which was visible in the tabloids.

David had been tracking what I wrote and said he'd really been looking forward to this, why hadn't we kept in touch anyway? Un-fucking-believable. I bit my tongue and said thanks for giving me an advantage over the other media; but then he said he didn't want to talk about his work. I could do an interview about the movie the next day. He wanted to catch up. I was exasperated but I couldn't resist. I was still an addict. We had drinks and I listened as he talked about himself and Hollywood. He didn't want to know what had happened to me, or he assumed he knew. No, he couldn't possibly assume that as no one was in touch with us both anymore. Anyone he might talk to about me wouldn't have heard directly from me for over a decade. Hearing him I realised he'd had an easier time than most who go to Hollywood thanks to landing his science fiction series very early on. So he'd been lucky. He felt right at home in the business and went to great parties. He was doing all the things he'd wanted to do. All the things he'd whispered in my ear in my bunkbed had come true for him. Per usual not any mention of any of the women he was sure to be sleeping with.

Somehow the conversation turned to something that reminded him of something from his childhood. He told the same story about the survival camp from the night we'd first met and I grasped he didn't remember how we'd bonded on that first day at university. I supposed it must be a stock story line from his repertoire. Despite that I was actually enjoying seeing him. Listening to him reminded me of why I'd never gotten over him. I loved the way he gestured, the way he spoke, the words he used and the way he analysed the situations and people he spoke about. No wonder he hadn't had too much difficulty getting an acting job in the most competitive town on the globe. I wondered if maybe the tone of his voice was in a timbre I might be genetically predisposed to like. He must've taken a cue from my face as then, to me it seemed to be out of the blue; he closed the space between us and lent over to kiss me.

At first I couldn't help myself. It was like finally having a glass of cool water after walking all day under hot sun. The smell of his skin ignited an instinctual response from my body. I relaxed to let the relief and peace wash over me. But then he started taking my shirt off and alarms started going off in my brain. As I braced and tried to push him away I said "wait, no." "Come on Cherie, I've been thinking about this for weeks now. What, do you have a boyfriend? Would he care?" David hadn't eased his hold and rather than back off he'd leaned in closer. I straightened my shirt and tried to sit upright but he still had his arms around me. I said "No, but I don't think this is a good idea. Haven't I seen somewhere you do actually have a girlfriend?" He'd understood from what I said there was no one else on my side. "Oh, you know what the rags are like; constantly making things up to sell copy." Suddenly I felt angry frustration. I thought no matter what the truth was he'd hide it because he'd never been sincere with me at any point in the history between us. Pretty much every emotion he'd expressed had turned out to be a con in light of what he'd actually done behind my back and who he'd chosen to respect publicly. Probably those were all cons too; just more artful ones.

I highly doubted a guy like David had nothing going on but decided that didn't actually matter. If he'd wanted something sincere with me he'd have said. He'd have spoken about what had happened between us. But he hadn't; he'd blown that off like we'd simply drifted apart rather than acknowledge any of the reasons we stopped speaking to each other. I wondered if he'd started that way would I have believed his explanations? Or would I have taken it as a tactic to make me drop my guard. I growled at him. "Whatever, why are you doing this now? Is there no one else that will sleep with you in this town? Did you run out of numbers to call in greater Atlanta?"

He looked at me with a bit of shock but more like he was pissed off. "Cherie's a bitch now? When did that happen? You've always been such a good girl." Then after a pause and some recomposure: "Cherie, your body shouldn't go to waste. You're the only one that ever got me really hard." He was smiling at me like nothing was wrong; like we were lying together on the top bunk before I learned he was with so many others at the same time. He was grinning at me like I was being a silly cow because he knew I wanted to give in to my desire. It was true, I really did want to but I couldn't stand the pain it would bring and I didn't want to risk a disease. I breathed deep and said "that's great to know David but I can't do this if it doesn't mean anything to you, that I can pretty clearly tell it doesn't. I'm not like you that way."

"Cherie you're killing me. When did you become such a prude?" There was no thought put into my reply. It simply flew out in a low hoarse whisper: "When you gave me gonorrhoea and chancroid and got me pregnant just before deciding you needed to be with Antra because she really got you." He was clearly baffled as he snarled "What? What are you talking about? Pregnant?" Shit, I hadn't meant to let that out. I thought he may well be just as angry at me for hiding it all this time as I was at him for all his cheating and mind games. Does a man have a right to know such things from a person they walked over then discarded without any remorse? I thought any person would be sad to know they'd lost a child and whatever else had happened between us I hadn't ever wanted to call up just to make him suffer. I figured there are probably millions of men in the world that don't care to know what happens with the women they leave behind. It's a joke to most men when they say they have "x" many kids that they know about. But it had come out so now I had to come clean. I braced myself and told him slowly but with composure. But I also didn't want there to be any confusion about what had actually happened if I was finally telling him. "That first summer of college I had a miscarriage on the same day you were getting a blowjob from Antra. You'd gotten me pregnant toward the end of the term but I lost it at about 8 weeks because of the STDs you gave me before the spring semester was over. I never told you because I didn't think you knowing that would help anything or anyone other than myself. You didn't seem to even own having given me STDs when I told you about that; despite you having been my only partner and that you damn well knew." His reply was this: "Jesus, that was really lucky huh? We were so young that would have fucked our lives for sure, or at least yours right?"

Right there, that second, I was finally able to make my heart fall in line with my head. The charm and the power over me disappeared. I was sitting on the couch looking at an asshole that probably had HIV and if not was surely lucky. Probably not actually; he was always lucky and agile enough to avoid any real consequences for anything. I'd just told him about the most heart-breaking episode of my life; that was directly the consequence of his actions, and he acted like it was no big deal. I wondered if he'd really understood what I said but knew that of course he'd understood. He simply didn't care because it didn't serve him.

I pushed him back and said "Sorry David, I can't do this. I've got to go." I was angry with myself again. Why the fuck was I apologising to him for refusing him? I said "I'll see you in my movie interview slot tomorrow with your agent; and after that I think we probably won't see each other ever again." He tried to pull me back down to the couch but I yanked myself away practically screaming "NO" then walked out of the room. I didn't hear if he said anything at all as I walked out. All I could see was the elevator, that lucky for me was opening just as I came to it; but I didn't hear the noise elevators make when their doors open. My mind was shutting down. I got into it quickly before anything might've happened to change my mind or allow him to add anything more.

The interview slot next day didn't happen because his agent called to cancel saying he'd unfortunately been double booked and they couldn't make it work. I wrote the piece I'd been assigned using the press release and what he'd yammered on about while we'd had drinks before he'd become physical. That was indeed the last I ever saw him in person. The movie I'd been there to interview him about was a blockbuster so eventually his face was on my TV every hour or so for months on end as it rotated through fast food meal deals, themed holidays, chat show teasers and the obligatory movie promos. I refused to watch any chat show he was going to guest on. If he came up on the entertainment news I'd change the channel. My boss didn't know what the story was between us but my behaviour was clearly overt as he asked someone else to do future junkets David was scheduled to be at. Actually, it may have been instructions from David's agent that led to that, but I didn't care. No one asked me about it so I told no one.

As David became more famous I saw his face on posters, billboards, TV adverts, print adverts, cereal boxes and novelty items. Every time

I saw him my heart would flutter with shame and attraction at the same time. I'd feel anxiety that eventually – after several more years - died down from repetition but never entirely muted. I saw by accident in a weekly gossip mag when he started dating the woman he finally married. I debased myself by buying a copy so I could see the photos of the nuptials. She was a personal trainer that did a popular series of weight loss and toning videos.

When their first kid was born I read an interview where he said it had transformed his life and he'd never imagined what fatherhood could be. I thought well; obviously because he'd never cared to until it was convenient for him. I had come to realise after all those years I'd been in love with the American version of Alfie. I was just one poor sod in a long string of dupes that he trod on and, by suffering, provided him with a brief experience for an aside to camera. Thanks to his celebrity and money David got his happy ending. As his kids aged in the society reports that inevitably appeared in my news feeds I noted they were each consistently 15 to 20 pounds overweight; right up through college. I wondered what kind of a taskmaster their mother must be; given her own profession and David's well-kept frame, for them to rebel in such a way. Maybe she preferred them that way? Maybe something else went on behind their closed doors. Who knew but them. It was certainly beyond me.

After that day in the hotel I didn't feel ardour for David anymore, but I still couldn't feel it for anyone else. I suppose you get a finite number of love chits to spend in a lifetime and I'd gambled them all away on the wrong person at a young age. I knew what real love felt like so I knew full well I never felt anything close to it for anyone else. I didn't have confused or unsure feelings about anyone. No one else ever came even remotely near to rekindling the light in me.

Also, it's not that I felt it was too late. Finding another person to share my most intimate thoughts and feelings simply wasn't a possible reality. I have ideas and thoughts I don't hear expressed by others in any context. Usually 20 minutes into meeting anyone at all from any walk of life they will have told me how strange my ideas are and avow it must be my unusual upbringing. That is if they last 20 minutes without making faces and shuffling off to find the normal people. If I'd had a normal childhood my thoughts might be more main stream. But even that aside how could I ever be totally genuine with anyone if I didn't tell them the truth about my own personal history? How exactly do you bring up you suffered a relationship like what I had, without it reflecting poorly on your own character? But that is just theorising given I never found anyone attractive enough, or even similar enough mentally, to actually contemplate whether I should need to share such stories.

Because others around me didn't seem to have ever felt as deeply about anyone (or had settled without admitting it to themselves); they never seemed to understand why I chose to be alone. Never give up hope, never stop looking, keep your heart open, there's someone out there for everyone... All of that crap was spouted by people who were uncomfortable that another person was capable of living alone. I had come to terms with my life but others always had opinions to express about how I was overly choosy. Isn't that idea just a reflection of how many people settle for less than what they genuinely want? Being less than choosy means you might as well be with anyone that comes by. Divorce rates and my friend Dom proved, for me, settling really means you are just fooling yourself and making things more complicated further down the line. That is, unless you're the type of person who will hang on no matter what; rather than live alone. Such a desperate person is likely to stay in a shitty relationship much longer than is healthy for them. All these meddlers in my intimate emotional space seemed to have an agenda to validate their own poor life choices by making it obligatory for all around them to do the same as them. Eventually they tired of it and left me alone. It was less annoying for people to not bring it up than the platitudes of earlier years.

I am surely not the only one in the world though, right? I mean if people generally were actually so desperate that living alone wasn't survivable then singledom wouldn't be on the rise. Despite increasing economic difficulties and recent recessions and austerities across the western world; the number of single households is continually increasing. In the USA they represent nearly a third of all households. Most of those are comprised of people over 55; so they are people who chose it after failing at cohabitation. In London single households are approximately 30% of the total. In Scandinavia these figures jump to 35-40%. Even in Asia; that westerners tend to consider conservative given all the quaint historical films we've been fed, singledom is on the rise. People would seem to be more self-reliant when they have an education, their own ability to gain an income and a sense of self-worth. While governments may fret this means there are no social networks for them to fall back on; I think I pay taxes to my government so that social services will be there for me when I need them. Regardless; I do believe the idea that 30-40% of the households in developed countries are made up of people who are overly demanding when it comes to who they share their beds with is insulting our intelligence. Might not these be people that in earlier times would have been forced to endure unhappy lives due to circumstance or lack of economic independence? I am grateful for social evolution and the possibility of these people (and me) being free from oppressive home lives; for them being able to choose for themselves what they are willing to live with.

When you know what sincere devotion is, isn't the real cowardice settling for less or making someone else settle for you feeling less; just to have physical company? I think more people realise in this day and age it is better to be alone than in a forced companionship. If real love happens that's great but living together with another person is not something you should have to trade away your integrity or peace for.

By the way, I may not have passionate or amorous love in my life but I do have a lovely dog who gives me unconditional love and companionship. I have a circle of decent people to pass the time with when I want to, and I have my own house to come home to when I need to be alone. My favourite leisure activity is a high-risk sport that no one else I know from any era of my life is interested in. I'm grateful no one is wasting my free time making me do some other activity I don't actually like. My holidays are to places no one else I know would ever go; and I am glad I don't have someone holding me back from going to those places with their limited tastes or sense of adventure. I don't meddle in other's emotional lives as I like to treat people how I'd want to be treated. And thanks to Facebook I am back in touch with all of those people I had gotten away from to avoid thinking of David. I can see what runs through my friends minds at any time of the day from any spot on the globe. I can share what I'm doing just as they do. I may live by myself but I am certainly not alone.

This is not an autobiography. This is not a biography. This is a work of fiction; albeit the stories are genuine and they are recounted as honestly as I was able given each individual perceives their own reality and there can be no objective truth.

I realise many may read this printed work and think they vaguely recognize some of the episodes recounted. People may even think they identify a version of themselves somewhere. However; general legal disclaimers aside, I feel it necessary to plainly state that this is a work of fiction.

If it were an autobiography, I would have had to start the tale with years of enduring an abusive childhood. I would have had to explain how I was raised by a misogynist who did not know how to deal with having progeny unlike himself. How a psychopath and pathetic excuse for a man firmly sought to crush his child's independence, personality and spirit with every kick, punch and mind game. A man bereft of the ability to feel or appreciate any joy unless it derived from asserting his power or position. A man who would make Martina Cole's Phillip Murphy look like an amateur insofar as being able to hide his vicious sadistic nature from all outside his family; appearing to be a kindly, concerned, rational parent when it suited him. One who was belligerently intolerant of any opinion differing from his own and who only appreciated what he could get out of people; seeing every single human contact in his life as a transaction that he needed to be on the winning side of.

I would have to explain why and how I spent years bending over backwards, jumping through hoops and biting my tongue until the moment when I might escape the grasp of such a person and position myself to start a life I wanted. All the while having to endure chastisement from strangers or distant relatives who had no clue what happened behind closed doors. Frankly, ignorant fools who thought I was just a moody ungrateful teenager any moment I let my resentment show. The years of self-denial and being told my thoughts and feelings were not worth anything to anyone set the narrative for a lifetime of being walked all over by people who were in positions of perceived authority; whether they meant to taking advantage or not. Cervantes was right: if you pretend to be a thing long enough you are in danger of becoming it without realising. By the time I was near freedom I had lost the ability to stand up for myself or what I wanted. I had quite literally had my own volition beaten out of me and did not know how to say NO to anyone. I habitually did things I did not want to with better performance than people who actually wanted to be doing them.

If this were an autobiography I would have to tell you how, after counting down the days of the last separation from the love of my life like it was the timeline to my deliverance; he dumped me like yesterday's trash and (I thought then) never looked back. How the person I most trusted and loved in my life, the only person I had ever dared to genuinely trust unequivocally and who for me embodied sweetness and light and was the definition of care; force fed me poison against my express will to ensure the child inside me died. For the love of my life it was better to kill our baby than be tied to me or to my family in any way. He thought he knew better than me what suited me; and he believed it was to not drag him down by having his child. For me to have his progeny was not an option. It was a horror story for him to avoid. He'd looked me in the eye and said "you don't want to have my baby"; at which point a warm consuming glow of love shot from my belly to my heart and I knew that was the one thing I most wanted in the world. I sometimes wonder if it wasn't the baby trying to make me conscious and aware s/he was there; crying out for me to take care of it.

The father of my child saw in my eyes that I wanted it and that made him angry. Between having been trained to defer to the will of others and not being able to comprehend fully what he was doing - as it was an unimaginable act - until it was too late; I was defenceless against him when he did it. A lifetime of beatings had taught me to submit to aggression to minimise the wrath of the belligerent and his anger triggered a visceral obedience; although, I never fathomed he could so easily and completely destroy me. I was incapable of believing he could do me such harm until he had done it. Even as it happened I wasn't able to assimilate what he'd done into my consciousness. My rational mind left my brain and didn't come back for quite a while.

When I finally was able to fully realise what he had done it was as if hydrochloric acid burned the receptors in my brain where love might be felt. Nothing but malformed scar tissue remained and there was no way to regenerate the lost capability to love another. I look back on that day and wish I had not trusted him. I clearly was not intelligent enough to know who is trustworthy and who is not. I wish I had never believed he loved me. I was an idiot to have ever imagined I might be lovable to anyone. I wish I had not believed him to be a good person. How could a good person impose their will over another via murder of an innocent? I learned later that the kind of poison he'd used often killed the mother along with the child. I wished I had been that lucky. He negated my right to choose to have it. Why couldn't he simply have walked away and left me to have the child on my own? How is it possible that one's own baby be so anathema to their vision of the world that they feel the need to ensure it not be born; despite the wishes of the potential mother? In the 21st century I simply don't understand it. I wished I could change it. If I could I would scream in my younger self's ear to scratch and fight or to run, but the past is set.

The love of my life made me a pariah by telling everyone I knew that I had left him because I was a loose whore; despite nothing possibly ever being further from the truth. The death of what was inside me drove me mad and put me right back in the hands of the misogynist who'd raised me because I did not have the means to live independently. What happened to me would doubtless have scarred any "normal" person for life. Programmes like Oprah Winfrey's or indeed stories often told on the evening news prove most people do not get over such life events no matter how many years they live on after. Quite a lot of people who've suffered tragedies of such magnitude spend their lives medicated or in therapy. However; I knew from a lifetime of experience better than to confide to my father what had happened. Not having any understanding of my very human emotions and annoyed he was no longer able to manipulate me to his liking; my father then tried repeatedly to have me declared mentally ill. I was made to see many psychiatrists and psychologists and they all had the same advice: your grief is normal, get away from your family and never look back.

Life would have been less painful without the ever present knowledge that the person for whom I had the deepest and truest feelings of my life had found me so revolting, abhorrent and vile that I should not have his baby and that whether I wanted to or not had not been a factor for him to even consider. Every day I would wake up wishing that I had died instead of my unborn child. Every day I would make myself go through the motions like I was a "normal" person but most of the time I felt like I should be getting a medal for managing to breath or put one foot in front of the other. Easier said than done to not look back, but for decades I blocked quite a bit from my consciousness in order to survive.

I did the best I could only to end up living in perpetual poverty; a slave to systems designed to favour those with inherited wealth that I did not have the benefit of. Over the years my sense of insignificance was confirmed and repeatedly reinforced as the people I came into contact with in all the limited spheres of my life demonstrated clearly they only cared about what I could do for them and hang the effect it might have on me. With no family to speak of and no friends to watch my back I was an ingénue at the mercy of luck who still did not know how to say NO; although I did develop the ability to leave a place when I was on the brink of annihilation.

Two thoughts permeated my existence: I was an aberration that should not have offspring and whatever I might want was irrelevant to the person to whom I'd entrusted my own life. For decades I could not stand to see other people with children because the sight of them always reminded me that I did not deserve to have any. I was not allowed to have a child because I was a waste of flesh and energy. I could not be near children because I might taint them with my presence. The one person I had truly loved betrayed me in the worst way I could imagine, even after years of turning it over in my mind; and I knew in the centre of my soul this could only be my own fault. I did not have the presence of mind to recognise bad character so how could I ever be allowed to be responsible for the wellbeing of another? I couldn't even defend or take care of myself.

That same love of my life married a woman who; when she found out she was pregnant, ran to me to say she did not want his child and did not want to spend her life with him. When she said that I lashed out and told her if she didn't disappear from my sight I'd rip her eyes out of their sockets. I gratefully didn't see her again for eight years; when she turned up in a place she didn't belong to tell me she knew what he'd done to me and every last detail of what had happened between us. She thought it was just fine given what an ugly fat cunt I was. I couldn't argue with her. That time I simply turned around and left the place I was. I actually left the country the next day. There was nothing to keep me anywhere and no one who gave a shit if I stayed or went.

At a much older age and by absolute chance I ran into that same love of my life only to discover he'd wasted years on drugs, self-destruction and empty relationships trying to drown his all-consuming guilt; before settling on the next woman he'd knocked up. Through it all he'd never thought to speak to me about it though. Why should he have? He said he felt sorry for what he'd done; or maybe he just felt sorry for himself. He also insisted he had not made any mistake that critical day that devastated my life, so it was clear where I stood just not why he cared if he'd made no mistake. He'd lived the life he'd promised me with the stupid cow who didn't want his child. He hadn't force-fed her poison, and hadn't let her end her pregnancy either. The arrogant twat that was insecure enough to seek me out to insult me was who he'd thought was good enough to have his children. He'd spent over a decade trying to prove to himself that habit and obligation can replace true feelings if you pretend long enough; only to realise he was living a sham he felt unable to extricate himself from.

Between what his wife had said to me all those years ago and what he said then; I realised I must be the elephant in his bedroom. Despite saying he believed it wasn't a mistake, he had never forgiven himself for what he'd done to me. He admitted cowardice and I realised he'd lashed out like a hurt child unaware of the true meaning of his actions until the aftermath. Having seen what life was with someone he didn't truly love he must've wondered at what it could've been if he hadn't snuffed his own first child. If he had lived what life had put in front of him rather than run like a coward from his own heart. But his world was too narrow and he was too old and tired to start again. Try as I did to hate him I could only feel sorrow for his self-loathing and pusillanimity in living a lie. Compassion stopped me from telling him that I had lost the will to live the day he'd killed my baby and nearly killed me. Every single time I remember that day I feel the pain all over again. Only thinking I am lucky not to have been born in the Congo or in Asia makes me realise how small my own suffering is compared to what most women's lives are in this modern world.

Perhaps someday I may write the autobiography that this is not. I suppose that depends on how many people are disposed to read this work of fiction.

I just want to be clear that this is not an autobiography or a biography; though the stories in it are indeed true and it is wholly written from the heart.

A SELECTION OF SONGS BY THE JIMJAMS

My Love is a Dove

My love is a dove
Who hovers and covers my hope
Like soap he washes
The splotches of reality from my sanity

Yet he rarely acts fairly
For he believes in what he sees as just
But he must be wrong
For my song is drowned out by his bout
With my independence in reference to my life
It causes my strife

My love is a dove
Who hovers and covers my hope
Like soap he washes
The splotches of reality from my sanity

I'm selfish you'll say
And it may be so but so is he
He wants to control my role as a person and block me
Now you think how can this fink be my love?
Such is above my understanding
My standing on the subject is to reject this boy
Who really needs a toy not a woman or a human
I begin to see that to be free I must leave him
To swim in his own sea then I will be free

My love is a dove
Who hovers and covers my hope
Like soap he washes
The splotches of reality from my sanity

LOVE HOLE

I sit in my room humming a sad tune
While some pale grey thoughts float round in my head
They collect in spots that I'd thought were dead
I don't understand why this emotion will not leave me

My mind is a hole fifty feet deep
Into it my emotions will seep
And when the most feared
Have at last disappeared
I'll be free and perhaps I'll sleep

I know in my mind a silly notion is all it is
See, I know better now…
Through pain's teaching I learned how to survive
Good will never come if it is alive in your poor poor heart

My mind is a hole fifty feet deep
Into it my emotions will seep
And when the most feared
Have at last disappeared
I'll be free and perhaps I'll sleep

When hurt and tears come
It is surely the start
That is how I learned that if one must love
It is best to love indifference best

My mind is a hole fifty feet deep
Into it my emotions will seep
And when the most feared
Have at last disappeared
I'll be free and perhaps I'll sleep

<u>Sick</u>

What do you think of me?
Or do you ever?
My heart has broken

My love is not beautiful
It is murderous painful
Tearing me to shreds
My love is not bountiful
It paralyses my soul
Any colours turn to dark reds
It eclipses my conscious
It feeds on my tired heart

I think of you
The way you speak
Kisses sweet but few
The loving feel of you

My love is oblivious
To my suffering apart
For freedom I cannot vie
Without my love I die

You must know the way I feel
I need you now
In my soul I know
You do realise your effect on me
Perhaps you care? Do you dare?

What do you think of me?
Or do you ever?
My heart has broken

WHAT IS LOVE

What is love?
Love is what I feel for you
But love; what is it?

It makes my flesh cry out in the middle of the night
Clamouring for your touch which it will never feel
Screaming ever louder at the injustice it endures
Being kept so far away from you
So loud I wonder how the howling doesn't wake up the world

It makes the core of my existence want to mingle with yours
Coming to attention at the sight of you
Trying to escape the confines of my body
Enraged at its powerless attempts to reach you
To be with you
Rattling my ribcage wrenching my heart

What is love?
Love is what I feel for you
But love; what is it?

It makes me wary trying to hide what
I know you know
Alarmed I might startle you
Paralysed should you spring away

It makes my soul want to die
Not to have to stand anymore
Yet I endure despite my weakness
Despite my emptiness despite myself
I go on enduring wondering at it all
Wondering how I am able

But love; what is it?
It is the poison that keeps me alive
Allowing me to feel its strength
The violence that holds me
Keeps me under duress
Love is you
Love is you
Love is you

RAIN

As the birds in the sky
So bright and blue
And the flowers on the trees
That remind me of you
With the rain I will be

The rain that falls
So pure to the ground
And the patter it makes
Blends with all other sound
Bringing life around it
While my sorrow it takes

I wish the rain would stay today
Stay here with me and peace
For by tomorrow peace will have fled
And my hope by then will cease
A hope that life can be wonderful
And that people can be led by joy

We are sitting in a new feeling car on the wrong side of the road; unless you live on a British island, and I am driving. It's a beautiful warm sunny day; but not too bright, and the trees are green. It is quiet and there's no traffic. There is a dual carriageway in front of us.

I turn to him and ask "sweetie, do you have the map? I'm not sure which way we're meant to be going now." He's staring at me but not reacting. He looks confused and a surprised. "Sweetie, are you ok? You look stunned. I think the map is here."

I reach over to the passenger side sun visor and pull it down. Doing so my upper body is right by his. The map is in a net on the back of the visor and I start to take it out when he grabs me and hugs me close. It's a sudden action like he's been overcome by something he was fighting. I feel happy for the first time in a VEEERRRRY LOOOOOONG time.

So happy.

Finally.